# GHOSTLY ASYLUM

*A Harper Harlow Mystery Book Seven*

## LILY HARPER HART

HarperHart Publications

# ONE

"Don't move!"

Harper Harlow swiped at her grimy face, wiping away the dirt that had accumulated when her partner Zander Pritchett decided – in his infinite wisdom, of course – to help her capture the Jenkins ghost by hopping in her path and declaring that he was her protector.

They'd been best friends since kindergarten so Harper was used to Zander's grand gestures, but she couldn't help but internally lament the fact that he always seemed to pick the exact wrong time to unleash his inner guardian.

"Does it look like I'm going to move?" Zander pinned Harper with a disgusted look as he ran his hand through his filthy hair, making a face when he detected something he was fairly certain came with creepy-crawlies attached to it. They stood in the middle of an abandoned barn on the outskirts of Whisper Cove, a real estate developer hiring their company Ghost Hunters, Inc. – or GHI to those lucky enough to be a part of the inner circle – to clean out the ramshackle building so they could tear it down and erect new condominiums. It seemed whenever the workers approached with their equipment they

were attacked by an unseen force that hurled rotten fruit from the nearby apple tree at them. It happened with enough regularity that they got antsy and hired professionals.

That's what Harper and Zander were. Professionals. They were professional ghost hunters, which earned snickers from some people and respect from others. They were used to both so they didn't pay much heed to what others thought about them.

"I didn't think you were going to move last time and yet you did," Harper said dryly, pulling a slice of rotten apple from the ends of her shoulder-length blond hair. "Ugh. I don't even like apples."

"Who doesn't like apples?"

"Um ... me."

"I don't think that's true." Zander always chose the oddest time to pick a fight and this was no exception. He couldn't see and talk to ghosts like his best friend, but the flying fruit unnerved him all the same. When he was unnerved, he liked to talk. "You like apple pie."

He had a point, Harper internally conceded. She did like apple pie. "Perhaps I only like cooked apples."

"That's a little sad." Zander rolled his neck as he peered through the hole in the barn wall. He'd lost track of the happy rotten apple thrower a few minutes before. "Where do you think he went?"

"Not far." Harper leaned forward a bit so she could scan the gloom. The barn was essentially falling down around them. One stiff breeze is all it would take to topple the structure. While the real estate developer might be happy with that outcome, Harper knew that didn't mean the ghost would flee the area. Instead, the displaced spirit was far more likely to up the apple-throwing angst – perhaps opt for bricks if they were handy – if that happened. "I think he's been here for a very long time."

Harper hadn't been able to get a clear view of the ghost as of yet – she didn't need to know what he looked like to help him pass to the other side – but she was fairly certain he was big ... and ornery.

"What was your first clue?" Zander deadpanned. "Was it the fact that the barn has been sitting out here alone, rotting, since before we were born? Or is it the fact that I'm pretty sure I heard him whisper a gay slur when he buzzed past me ten minutes ago?"

Harper stilled, surprised. "He whispered at you?"

Zander jutted out his lower lip and nodded. "He's mean."

Harper didn't doubt that the ghost was mean. He was throwing fruit, for crying out loud, of course he was mean. She'd never known Zander to be able to hear a ghost when she couldn't, though. In fact, there were times Zander swore up and down he didn't hear Harper when she talked ... especially when she said something he didn't want to hear. She couldn't help being a bit suspicious.

"Did he really say something to you or are you just projecting because that girl at the coffee place this morning commented that gay guys always have the best shoes?"

Zander pursed his lips. "You can't tell just by looking at me that I'm gay," he exploded.

"I agree." Harper's lips curved. "I think you're the manliest man on the planet. The fact that you have great shoes is simply an added bonus. You shouldn't take it personally."

"Whatever." Zander made an exaggerated face. "She just assumed I was gay because of my new Sperry Topsiders and that's just ... very judgmental. Peach is in this season."

"Of course it is." Harper absently patted Zander's arm. She was used to his dramatic meltdowns. Heck, she even enjoyed them on occasion. Now wasn't the proper time for him to devolve into one of his patented freakouts, though. "She was clearly evil, Zander. Those little unicorn clips in her hair should've tipped you off."

"You know how I hate unicorns," Zander hissed. "People think they're magical and fight on the side of good, but I know better."

"Yes, you know better than everyone." Harper narrowed her eyes when she caught a hint of movement in the barn. "I think he's over there."

Zander followed her gaze, knitting his eyebrows as he stared. "I'm still going to place a wager that the ghost is a judgmental jerkwad."

"Because he comes from a less enlightened time?"

"Because he throws fruit," Zander snapped. "Only a douche would throw fruit."

Harper couldn't argue with that. "Definitely." She bobbed her head as she came up with a plan. "Okay, here's what's going to happen, I'm going to venture out into the middle of the barn and draw him to me. When I give you the signal, you need to throw out the dreamcatcher as close to my feet as possible. Do you understand?"

Zander's face was a mask of indignation as he crossed his arms over his chest. "Do I understand? We've been doing this for years. Of course I understand. I'll throw out the dreamcatcher, you'll lead him across it and he'll be magically transported to the other side."

That wasn't exactly how it worked, but Harper wasn't in the mood to argue with him, especially since he seemed primed to model for the foldout in the newest edition of Petulant Quarterly.

"Aim for the spot right in front of my shoes," Harper pressed. "It's important."

"I've got it!"

"Whatever." Harper rolled her eyes as she stood. "Whatever you do, don't move."

"Oh, geez." Zander slapped his hand to his forehead. "I hate it when you talk down to me. Next thing I know you'll be making fun of my shoes."

"Oh, those shoes are too fabulous," Harper teased, readying herself. "I would never make fun of those shoes. Ready? Here I go."

**"WHAT PART OF** 'don't move' did you have trouble grasping?"

Harper was in a foul mood by the time she swung into the small office space they rented to serve as an office for GHI two hours later. She was even dirtier than before and she was almost certain that the apple chunks in her hair were starting to ferment.

"I didn't move," Zander barked. He was equally as filthy and he wanted to head home rather than to the office, but she insisted they had to stop in long enough to update their co-workers and make sure they sent out the bill before calling it a day.

"You did, too."

"I did not."

"You did, too."

"I did not."

"Guys!" Molly Parker, GHI's lone paid intern, clapped her hands to get Zander and Harper's attention as they trudged through the office. She sat at the front desk, a bright-eyed man and fresh-faced woman sitting across from her, and she looked unbelievably frustrated.

"What?" Harper asked, refusing to apologize for her unprofessional entrance. If the new people were clients and they didn't like her attitude ... well ... they could just bite the smelly apples and find someone else to hunt ghosts for them. *And good luck with that because no one else will want the job.*

"This is Michael Knox and Lucy Bush," Molly explained, her short green hair gleaming under the pink gel lights Zander insisted they install in the main office because he refused to risk falling into bad lighting when he was trying to impress potential clients. "They work for that ghost show on television."

Harper stilled, surprised. Whatever she was expecting, that wasn't it. "Ghost show?"

The man who Molly introduced as Michael Knox hopped to his feet and extended his hand. "That's right. I'm the producer of *Phantoms* on IGH."

While most people would have no idea what IGH was, Harper couldn't help but perk up at mention of the network. "Independent Ghost Hunters Network," she mused, working overtime to adjust her attitude. These were fellow colleagues, after all. "We watch that channel all of the time in our house."

"Oh, you're a couple?" Michael's expression was friendly as he returned to his seat. "That must be why you were arguing. Most people find they can't work and play together without the occasional meltdown."

"We *live* together," Harper corrected. "We don't play together."

"We played 'the last one who puts something in the trash has to take it to the curb' just last night," Zander countered, his annoyance evident. "How dare you say we don't play?"

Harper reclaimed a bit of her anger and flicked her eyes to her best friend. "I'm going to play with the idea of putting my foot in your behind if you're not careful."

"Oh, let it go." Zander rolled his eyes to the heavens. "It's not my fault you tripped over your own feet and got pelted with another round of rotten apples. How can you possibly blame me for that?"

"It's actually easier than you think," Harper replied, not missing a beat. "I told you not to move and you moved."

Zander planted his hands on his narrow hips. "I did not move!"

"You did, too. Twice."

"Guys!" Molly was at the end of her rope as she stood. Her short-cropped hair was always changing color so Harper and Zander were used to it, but the green washed out her features in such a manner that Harper thought the young girl looked sick. Harper couldn't wait for the inevitable change when it came.

"I'm sorry." Harper held up her hand in a placating manner as she forced a smile. "You caught us at a bad time. We just completed a rather ... difficult ... job and we're both tired."

"Not so tired that we can't talk about being on television," Zander said, shifting gears almost immediately. It took him longer than it should have, but he'd finally put together why the producer of *Phantoms* was in their office. "That's why you're here, right? You want to put us on television, don't you?"

"I do indeed." Michael beamed at Zander. "We want to film an episode locally and we were asking around about guides and your name came up with some regularity."

Harper didn't consider herself cynical by nature – at least not all of the time, that is – but she couldn't help being suspicious. "You asked around and our names came up with regularity? May I inquire who you asked?"

"Does that matter?" Zander widened his eyes, something unsaid passing between him and Harper as he attempted to retain control of the conversation.

Harper refused to back down. "It matters to me."

"That's because you're a whiner," Zander muttered. "You whine about people moving – even though they clearly didn't move – and you whine about one of the best television shows ever recognizing our talents and offering to make us stars."

Harper maintained a neutral expression, but just barely. "I'm pretty sure that's not what they offered."

"That's what I heard."

"That's not even remotely what he said."

Michael cleared his throat to break up the potential fight. Harper was convinced he was about to explain that he'd made a huge mistake and excuse himself, but instead he did the exact opposite. "You guys are going to be perfect for what we're planning. You might very well be stars by the end of the episode. Don't you think so, too, Lucy?"

The woman, a bright-eyed beauty with long auburn hair and a pristine smile, immediately started bobbing her head. "They're fantastic. They have great natural chemistry. Our viewers are going to love them."

"More importantly, they're going to laugh with them," Michael said, his eyes never leaving Harper's face. "You're perfect."

Zander crossed his arms over his chest, smug. "See. We're perfect."

Harper liked a compliment as much as the next person, but she wasn't an easy mark. "And what are we perfect for?" she asked, refusing to let the conversation get away from her before she had a chance to see the entire picture.

"We have a special trip planned to the Ludington Asylum," Michael explained. "We've been scouting the location and doing a great deal of research and it's supposed to be absolutely teeming with ghosts. Have you heard of it?"

Harper's heart rolled at mention of the asylum.

"Of course we've heard of it," Zander enthused. "It's supposed to be the most haunted place in Michigan. It's only about an hour and a half away. We wanted to visit as teenagers, but we couldn't find anyone to drive us out there."

"My understanding is that the asylum is located on a small island." Lucy furrowed her brow as she flipped through a file. "How could you drive out there if it's on an island?"

"I should've said motor," Zander corrected. "My uncle has a boat and we tried to pay him to take us, but he refused. He doesn't believe in ghosts and yet even he heard the stories about the asylum and he didn't think we would be safe."

"Yes, from everything we've heard the spectral energy at that location is supposed to be phenomenal," Michael enthused. "Since no one visits the property, it's an untapped resource and we want to be the ones to tap it."

"You're an untapped resource, too," Lucy added. "You guys have built up quite the reputation in ghost-hunting circles and we want to be the ones to introduce you to the world. We want to be the ones to tap you first."

"Did you hear that, Harp? They want to tap us." Zander was beyond giddy. He was so far gone he didn't recognize the double entendre. If he'd been in full charge of his faculties he would've made a hundred jokes before letting it slide.

"I heard." Harper scratched her chin as she internally debated the scenario. "I'm going to need some more information before we agree to anything."

"Of course." Michael's smile was so large it almost swallowed his entire face. "I'm sure money is an issue."

"Money *is* an issue," Harper agreed. "I also want to know what kind of security you'll have in place and any contingency plans in case we need to flee from the island."

Michael's eyebrows hopped up his forehead. "Flee?"

"The island is supposed to be treacherous," Harper supplied. "We've heard stories for years about it. Some people have disappeared while trying to visit and never been found. Scoff if you want, but that's happened at least two times."

"She's not wrong," Zander hedged, returning to reality. "We have heard a lot of funky stories about that island."

"We'll have a security team in place," Michael supplied. "You'll be perfectly safe. We brought a contract for you to sign if you're interested. It's pretty basic but ... I'm sure you'll want to look it over."

"We definitely will," Harper agreed.

"And then we'll sign on the dotted line." Zander was back to being giddy. "We're going to be on television, Harp. Can you believe it?"

Harper couldn't quite believe it. She also refused to agree until she ran the idea past one other person. "I want to talk to Jared, too."

Zander's smile slipped. "Oh, geez. Captain Killjoy is going to veto the idea right out of the gate. Why would you want to do that?"

"Because I want to hear what he has to say." That was the truth, although Harper also wanted to give herself a bit of time to absorb the idea before agreeing to it. "We need to look over the contract and talk to a few people but ... we'll be in touch."

# TWO

"There's my favorite girl."

Jared Monroe let himself into Harper's bedroom shortly after finishing his shift at the Whisper Cove Police Department. It had been a boring day – two jaywalkers and a property dispute by a divorcing couple that turned into a public scene in the middle of Main Street – and he was looking forward to spending a romantic evening with his ladylove.

Instead of greeting him with a bright smile and enthusiastic hug, like she usually did, Harper stared through her bedroom window.

"What's wrong?" Jared was instantly on alert. He met Harper the previous spring, when the trees were just coming into full bloom, and now that the leaves were beginning to turn as autumn hit he felt as if he'd known her his entire life. He'd become very familiar with her moods.

"What do you mean?" Harper forced her gaze from the window and offered up a wan smile. "Why do you naturally assume something is wrong?"

"Because Zander isn't in the kitchen cooking a big dinner and you're hiding in here," Jared replied. He knew better than getting in the middle of a fight between Harper and her best friend, but he wasn't keen on sitting through an uncomfortable evening if they were in the middle of one of their notorious fights. "What happened?"

"Well, for starters, I told Zander not to move and he did ... twice ... and I got pelted with rotten fruit for half the afternoon."

"That would explain why you've showered." Jared shuffled closer, running his fingers through Harper's damp hair. "It looks like you've taken care of that problem, though."

"You should've smelled me an hour ago."

"I was looking forward to nothing else all day." Jared's grin was contagious because Harper couldn't stop the corners of her mouth from tipping up. "In fact, I sat at my desk doing a ridiculous amount of paperwork and my mind kept drifting to exactly when I would be able to sniff you."

"Ha, ha." Harper poked Jared's side. "I told him not to move."

"Yes, well, it sounds as if you've had a difficult day." Jared navigated Harper to the bed so they could get comfortable. If it led to something else after they talked, he wasn't opposed to that either. Given her mood, though, he knew he would have to drag her out of her doldrums before they got to the fun part of their evening. "You usually don't let Zander's hijinks derail you like this, though. That makes me think something else is going on."

Harper's expression was rueful as she settled next to him, enjoying the way Jared's hand automatically went to the tense spot on the back of her neck. He dug his fingers in and began to massage, hoping to loosen up her mouth as well as her muscles.

"You read me pretty well," Harper supplied. "Before Zander, no one read me as well as you."

"I'm going to take that as a compliment even though you know how much I hate being compared to Zander."

"He's angry with me."

"Ah." *Now we're getting somewhere,* Jared internally mused. "Why is he angry with you? Does he smell like rotten apples, too?"

"I washed my hair," Harper complained. "You shouldn't be able to smell it."

"It's very faint. Don't worry about it. I happen to love the smell of apples."

"I only like apples when they're cooked in a pie. That's something else I discovered today."

"So you have had a busy day," Jared teased, tickling her ribs. He didn't like how tense she was. Whatever was bothering her was bigger than she wanted to let on. Or perhaps she didn't even realize how agitated she was. It wouldn't be the first time her emotions took hold before her brain caught up.

"Yeah." Harper chewed on her lip as her expression darkened. "There were two people in the office when we got back."

"Okay." Jared waited for her to tell the story in her own way. If he needed to step in, make his presence known because someone was threatening her, he would do it without hesitation. It took him a bit to grasp the fact that she really did talk to ghosts, but he believed it with his whole heart now. If someone was going after her because of that ... well ... it wouldn't end well for that individual.

"Michael Knox and Lucy Bush."

"Are those names supposed to mean something to me?" Jared asked, legitimately curious. He'd only been in Whisper Cove for six months, but he thought he knew all of the locals. Neither name sparked recognition.

"I don't know. I thought you might." Harper shifted on her hip, her fingers moving to Jared's toned stomach so she could trace his abs through the shirt. "They work for IGH."

"I don't know what that is."

"Independent Ghost Hunters Network."

Jared knit his eyebrows as he racked his brain. "Is that the channel you and Zander watch when you want to make fun of how other people hunt for ghosts?"

Harper nodded. "Michael Knox produces the show *Phantoms,* and Lucy Bush is the woman who does the interviews and narration."

"Ah. Okay. I can't say I know who she is, but I'm sure I'd recognize her if you pointed her out. You've made me sit through hundreds of those shows."

"I haven't made you sit through them," Harper clarified. "I invited you to hang out with me while I did it. There's a difference."

Her feisty attitude returned a bit, which made Jared grin. "Thank you for the clarification."

"You're welcome." Harper rested her chin on Jared's chest and bit back a sigh as he stroked the back of her head. He was blessed with infinite patience – something she wasn't used to because everyone else in her life, including her parents, was something of a spaz. She needed that patience now because she was having trouble sorting through her emotions.

"Do they want to film you?" Jared asked.

Harper's eyebrows hopped. "How did you know that?"

"It's the only thing that made sense. Plus, I'm a detective." He playfully tapped his temple.

"Right." Harper snuggled closer. "They do want to film us. They want to do an episode featuring us."

"And you don't want to be on television?" Jared didn't want to voice his concerns until she'd already expressed hers. He wasn't sure how he felt about his girlfriend being on a television show, but the network wasn't exactly popular and it's not as if Harper would pick up thousands of fans by doing it. Plus, well, it ultimately wasn't his decision. She had to decide and he would support her no matter what.

"I honestly don't know how I feel about that," Harper admitted. "I don't always look my best after a takedown."

"No one looks better than you. Ever."

"Cute."

"I do my best." Jared brushed his lips over Harper's forehead, doing his best to soothe her even though he wasn't yet aware why she was so bothered. "What does Zander think?"

"Oh, he's already picturing himself going to ghost conventions and posing for photos with his adoring fans."

Jared didn't bother hiding his smirk. "I can see that."

"I would do the show just for him because of that," Harper admitted. "It's not the show. Even if we look like idiots – which we do on a daily basis, so it's not a big deal – I would be okay with that if it made him happy."

"So what's the problem?"

"It's the place they want to go."

"And where is that?"

"Ludington Asylum."

The name meant absolutely nothing to Jared. He grew up on the west side of the state and wasn't familiar with a lot of the Whisper Cove landmarks and lore. "I didn't know you guys had an asylum. How did I miss that?"

"It's not in Whisper Cove," Harper clarified. "It's about an hour away, in the middle of the lake."

Jared shifted, confused. "The asylum is in the middle of the lake? How?"

"It's on a small island," Harper explained. "The Ludington Asylum was famous back in the day. It was built in the 1940s and there was a lot of fanfare when it happened."

"And you remember that because you were there? And here I thought you were young and fresh."

"Ha, ha." Harper rolled her eyes. "I did a lot of research about the asylum when I was younger because everyone whispered about it being haunted. I wanted to know more."

"Ah." Things clicked into place for Jared. "I get where you're going. Go back to the beginning, though. I'm listening."

"Are you done with your comedy routine?"

"For the moment."

Harper took her time and visibly swallowed. "They built the asylum on the island because it was only accessible by boat. They thought that would mean fewer escape attempts."

"I would think they'd have security at an asylum," Jared pointed out.

"I'm sure they did, but between the time the asylum opened and shut down in the early 1970s they housed more than crazy people there. Wait ... using the term 'crazy people' is probably offensive, isn't it?"

"Probably. I'm not offended, though."

"I should've learned my lesson after this morning," Harper muttered. "By the way, if you don't want to get on Zander's bad side, don't point out that his new Sperry Topsiders look like the chosen footwear of a gay man. He's in a mood about that."

"You mean the peach boat shoes that make me think Sonny Crocket would've been jealous ... and taking notes?"

Harper snorted. "Sonny Crocket. Good reference. Zander loves that show."

"I loved that show, too," Jared noted. "I wanted to be a vice cop and live in Miami for a time because of it."

"If that happened we never would've met."

"So it clearly wasn't my destiny." Jared pressed Harper close and gave her a soft kiss. "Go back to the asylum."

Harper shook herself out of her reverie. "Right. You have to remember that back in the day they didn't have the medical standards and regulations they do now. People were locked up for weird things back then – things that very clearly aren't mental challenges – and they were treated in abhorrent ways."

"Like electroshock therapy?"

"Among others," Harper replied. "Homosexuality, for example, was considered a mental defect and a lot of patients were treated with aversion therapy."

"Which is?"

"They would be given a medication to make them sick to their stomach, shown a bunch of same-sex photos and movies, and then forced to throw up while watching."

Jared was horrified. "Seriously?"

"It's not just that," Harper said. "Women were sometimes locked up for having PMS, which was essentially a way for a man to get rid of his wife without killing her. He had all the power and could lock her up on just his word and there wasn't anything she could do about it."

"I guess that means I can't lock you in the closet next time you have PMS even if I mean it as a joke, huh?" Jared was teasing, but the story bothered him. "So you're saying the people who were locked up in this asylum didn't deserve to be there."

"No, that's not exactly what I'm saying," Harper clarified. "Some of the people sent there needed to be there. It's just, back then, they lumped all mental issues together. A woman who had mood swings was just as dangerous as a man who killed his wife and children."

Jared's hand tightened on the back of Harper's neck. "Oh. I get what you're saying."

"It was a different world," Harper said. "We think the practices they used back then sound barbaric now, but it was the norm. The Ludington Asylum was hardly the only facility using those methods."

"Okay, so I'm guessing it was shut down for good in the seventies. That's what you said, right?"

"It was, and that's when things really got out of control," Harper said. "The state shut down the hospital, but when they started going through patient records, they found a lot of them missing."

"Missing? The patients or the records?"

"Both. People apparently checked in, but they never checked out."

"So they were murdered there?" The more Jared heard about this asylum, the more he wanted to keep Harper from setting foot inside of it.

"No one knows. It's assumed some of them probably died of natural causes, but the doctor who ran the place disappeared right after it was shut down. To my knowledge, they never found him."

"I see." And, because he did, Jared couldn't stop his stomach from flipping. "So some of the missing patients might have died from natural causes, but there were probably too many of them for that to be completely true."

"Pretty much."

"So a lot of people died on that island," Jared mused. "Did they ever find the bodies?"

"Not that I heard of and given the size of the island – which I've only seen in photographs, mind you – I'm guessing they dumped the bodies in the water rather than deal with burying them."

"Well, great. That sounds nice and tidy." Jared ran his tongue over his lips as he considered Harper's conundrum. "You're worried the asylum is going to be so packed with ghosts it overwhelms you, aren't you?"

"Yes." Harper saw no reason to lie.

Jared went with his gut instinct. "So don't go."

"I've been leaning toward that decision myself."

"But?" Jared prodded. He knew it wouldn't be that easy.

"But Zander really wants to go," Harper replied. "Molly and Eric do, too." Eric was the fourth and final member of the GHI team, and although he hadn't been as excited as Molly, he voted with the others as soon as Michael and Lucy left the office a few hours before. "They think it sounds exciting."

"That's easy for them to say," Jared argued. "They don't see what you see."

"No, but ... I would be lying if I said I wasn't curious," Harper admitted. "I've always wanted to see the island. This could be my only chance."

"Or we can borrow Mel's boat one day next summer and I'll take you out there," Jared suggested. "We can spend an hour looking around at the grounds and give the building itself a wide berth."

"According to Michael Knox we'll be perfectly safe because our team and his team will meld. He also said he would have people ready to launch in rescue boats should something happen, although I'm not sure how feasible that is."

Jared wasn't convinced. "Heart, I don't want to tell you what to do, but this whole thing worries me. What if you're overwhelmed by this?"

"I'm not going to pretend it absolutely won't happen, but I don't believe it will," Harper replied. "I'm strong."

"You're the strongest person I know," Jared agreed. "That doesn't mean I like this idea."

"The thing is, if I don't go, I'm worried I'll always be haunted because I wasn't brave enough to try."

"Oh, geez." Jared pinched the bridge of his nose. "You've already made up your mind to do it, haven't you? I thought you were really leaning toward not doing it, but I was wrong."

"Part of me wanted you to talk me out of it," Harper conceded. "The thing is, I think I need to go."

"Need?"

Harper nodded. "I have to see or I'll always wonder."

Jared studied her face for a long beat, his nerves unsettled. Finally, he gave in. There was nothing else he could do. "Well, luckily for you

I've accrued some vacation time. If you're going to do this, I'm going with you."

Harper widened her eyes, surprised. "Really?" She didn't want to admit she was relieved. She never would've asked him to do anything of the sort. Once he volunteered his time, though, there was absolutely no way she intended to put up a fight. "That makes me feel better about things."

"I live to serve." Jared scooted lower on the bed and rolled Harper so she was on top of him. He used both of his hands to push her hair away from her face. "Did you really think I would let you go without me?"

Harper shrugged, noncommittal. "I didn't know. I can say that I've never been more relieved in my life. I'm not sure I could do this without you."

"Luckily for you, you don't have to find out." Jared wrapped his arms around Harper's slim back, sighing as she burrowed her head into his chest. "It might be fun, right?"

"We'll treat it like a romantic adventure."

"Yes, a romantic adventure where tortured ghosts will probably try to kill us," Jared muttered. "That sounds like the best vacation ever."

Harper tilted her head so she could lock gazes with him. "Have I mentioned that I love you?"

Jared's scowl slipped. "Not today."

"I do."

"I love you, too." Jared planted a scorching kiss on Harper's lips. "I think you should show me just how much."

"That's the plan."

The couple was just about to shift gears and shed clothes when the bedroom door burst open, allowing Zander entrance. His eyes flashed when he saw what Harper and Jared were about to do.

"Didn't we talk about knocking?" Jared challenged, dropping Harper's shirt to ensure she remained covered.

"Yes, but I heard the conversation through the heat vent and I didn't have time to knock in case you guys were already stripping," Zander replied. "For the record, I think you've made the right decision."

"Oh, well, good. I always base my decisions on what will make you happy," Jared drawled.

Zander ignored the sarcasm. "I have another good idea. I think I should bring Shawn along as extra security."

Shawn Donovan was Zander's new boyfriend. Since Zander had never made it to a third date with anyone else over the entirety of his dating history, Harper was fairly convinced that they were already serious despite only dating for a few weeks. Still, that didn't mean Shawn wouldn't serve as something of a distraction for Zander on the island.

"Can you focus on work if he's there?" Harper asked.

Annoyance flashed in Zander's eyes. "Of course."

"Well ... ." Harper chewed on her bottom lip as she feigned concentration.

"I think it's a good idea," Jared interjected. "That's one more person to act as security should it become necessary."

"See!" Zander jerked his thumb in Jared's direction. "Listen to Captain Killjoy. He knows what he's talking about."

"He's in," Harper said hurriedly, hoping to head off a fight between Jared and Zander. "I think it's a great idea. I was just messing with you."

Zander stared at Jared a moment longer before shifting his gaze to Harper. "That's good. I already invited him. He's looking forward to the trip."

Zander flashed a winning smile before turning on his heel and stalking out of the room. Jared watched him go with a mixture of relief and agitation.

"He could've at least shut the door," Jared muttered.

"I can't because dinner will be ready in ten minutes," Zander called from the hallway. "You can't get naked until you finish your dessert."

"Since when is that the rule?" Jared asked.

"Since I'm making blueberry pie."

"Oh, well ... ." Jared smiled at Harper. "I love you but ... blueberry pie."

"I've already been replaced in your heart," Harper lamented. "I can't believe it."

"You'll never be replaced in my heart," Jared promised. "It's just ... I love blueberry pie."

Strangely enough, Harper realized she was excited about the pie, too. "Will you still love me later? After the pie, I mean."

"I'm going to love you forever."

Harper found she believed him. "Me, too."

## 3

# THREE

"You're early."

Michael Knox stood on the dock next to a large boat, the morning sun peeking through the clouds, and pinned Harper with a bright smile. They were due to depart to the island within the hour, and after a busy previous day packing and shopping, Harper's group was packed and loaded for bear.

Er, well, for the most part.

"Most of us," Harper replied, returning the smile. "Zander and Shawn are a few minutes behind us. They have all of the food."

"The food?" Michael furrowed his brow, confused. "I said I would provide the food."

"Yes, but Zander doesn't roll that way," Jared interjected, his eyes busy as they roamed Michael's handsome face and broad shoulders. He realized he was taking stock as if Michael was competition – which was ridiculous – but he couldn't stop himself. "I'm Jared Monroe, by the way."

Michael shook Jared's extended hand. "Yes, Ms. Harlow mentioned she was adding a few people to her crew for this excursion. And what do you do for her?"

Jared flashed Harper a hot look before reminding himself that he should probably be somewhat professional given the fact that this trip could mean a lot for Harper's business prospects. "For this trip I'll be serving as security."

"This trip?"

"Jared is a police officer," Harper supplied, resting her hand on Jared's elbow in an effort to keep him tucked in at her side. "He's also my boyfriend."

"I see." Michael's expression didn't slip, but Jared was almost positive he saw a hint of disappointment flash in the depths of the man's eyes. "Well, I guess I can't blame you for not wanting to leave her alone with us Hollywood types."

"I never want to leave her alone," Jared said. "That's not the reason I'm tagging along, though."

Michael tilted his head, as if waiting for Jared to explain further. Instead Jared flicked his eyes to the parking lot where Eric and Molly were gathering coolers and bags from the back of Zander's car.

"Here comes the food," Jared said, his lips curving.

Michael widened his eyes when he realized exactly how many provisions Zander intended on bringing along for the trip. "Is he going to be serving five-course meals or something?"

"He just likes to be prepared," Harper explained.

"Oh, was he a Boy Scout?" Michael's expression was as innocent as the question, but Harper couldn't stop herself from snorting.

"Not exactly."

"He would never put up with the polyester blend of the shirt," Jared volunteered, smoothly sidestepping Harper's elbow when she moved to plant it in his stomach. "Hey, I was only speaking the truth."

Harper wanted to argue – and admonish Jared not to purposely push Zander's buttons – but they'd already had a long talk about this exact situation. Harper worried that, once they were trapped on a haunted island together, Jared and Zander would start snarking at one another and not stop until one of them was pecked to death.

"Is that everything?" Harper asked Zander as he approached.

Zander nodded, seemingly happy. "I have everything taken care of." He flashed a smile for Michael's benefit. "Just because we're going to be camping, that doesn't mean we have to eat bad food, right?"

"Um." Michael shifted his eyes to Harper, conflicted. "I guess not."

"It will be fine," Jared said, grabbing the end of the cooler Molly held and moving in tandem with Eric so they could load it on the boat. "There's no such thing as too much food when you're camping."

"I was just going to go the hot dog and potato chip route," Michael muttered, widening his eyes as Jared grunted to lift the cooler over the boat wall. "What did you bring?"

"Oh, a little of everything," Zander replied. "Don't worry. I have everything under control."

"He's a great cook," Molly enthused, her eyes going wide as she took in the boat. "Wow. I've never been on a boat this big before."

"Have you ever been on a boat?" Eric challenged, ice in his tone.

Harper darted her eyes in their direction, her antennae up. They'd been especially snippy with one another of late and she didn't know what to make of it. For months, Molly struggled with a heavy crush on Eric. He, in turn, had no idea she was alive because he had a crush on Harper. Once Jared got involved, Eric had a few bouts of attitude before conceding defeat. He'd been overly mean to Molly ever since.

"I've been on a boat," Molly fired back, her pert little nose wrinkling. "Of course I've been on a boat."

"Other than a bumper boat?" Eric pressed.

"I ... oh, shut up." Molly turned her attention to the equipment Eric packed and grabbed the biggest bag, groaning as she heaved it over her shoulder. "Other than a bumper boat?" she mimicked under her breath.

Harper pressed her lips together to keep from laughing. She could feel Michael's eyes on her and attempted to remind herself that she was supposed to be acting professional. "So ... where is the rest of your team?"

"They're checking out of the bed and breakfast we stayed at," Michael replied, seemingly relieved to have something to converse about that didn't revolve around Harper's emotionally dysfunctional team and their eating habits. "It's not like in bigger cities. We actually needed to check out rather than just leave. It was ... odd."

"Whisper Cove is stuck in the past," Harper supplied. "You get used to it after a bit."

"I guess that's true of any place." Michael rested his hip against one of the fence beams. "Did you ever consider moving on to a bigger area? Someone with your gifts would make a killing in a place like New Orleans."

"This is my home," Harper replied. "I don't want to leave. I mean, I don't mind visiting different places, but I can't ever picture myself living anywhere else."

"Well, it's a lovely area." Michael shifted his eyes to Jared as the police officer joined Harper on the dock. "And what about you, Mr. Monroe? Are you destined to stay in this area forever, too? I would think it's too ... small ... to keep your interest long term."

The question could've easily had two meanings, but Michael asked it in such an innocent manner that Harper couldn't decide if he meant to be a jerk or accidentally did it without realizing it.

"Oh, I love Whisper Cove," Jared said, rubbing his hand up and down Harper's back. "I have no intention of ever leaving."

"But surely you must want to move on to a bigger police department," Michael hedged.

"Maybe some day, but that day isn't today and that wouldn't force me to leave Whisper Cove," Jared said. "Most of the Michigan police departments don't have residency requirements. Plus, if I wanted to go to work for the sheriff's department or something down the line, I simply need to live in the county, not a particular community."

"Oh, yes, well ... I see you've given this some thought." Michael's smile was back in place. "Good for you."

Jared slid his arm around Harper's waist and anchored her snugly to his side. "It's definitely good for me."

Thankfully, at that moment, Michael's attention shifted to the parking lot. Apparently his team had arrived and he offered up a lame mumble before hurrying in their direction. Harper watched him go, amused, and waited until he was out of earshot before turning on Jared.

"What was that?"

Jared had the grace to be abashed, but only minimally. "He was hitting on you."

"He was not."

"He kind of was."

"He really wasn't."

"Well, he was doing something," Jared argued. "He's definitely interested in you. That's why he was trying to grill me about my future plans. I hate guys like him."

"Handsome men?" Harper's eyes lit with mirth as Jared scowled.

"Guys who think they can make other guys look bad in front of their girlfriends," Jared corrected. "By the way, I'm much more handsome than he is."

"You definitely are," Harper agreed, her gaze curious as she turned to watch Michael's team stride toward the boat. "What do you think of him?"

"I think he has excellent taste in women."

"Not that."

"I don't know what to think of him yet," Jared said. "He doesn't seem like a bad guy. He's a little pompous, don't get me wrong, but I think he's simply jaded by life."

Harper cocked an amused eyebrow. "Jaded by life?"

"He seems to expect women to fall at his feet," Jared explained. "When you didn't, that only served to rev up his interest."

"Is that like some testosterone thing?"

"Pretty much," Jared confirmed. "By the way, if he doesn't take heed of the obvious warning signs – and soon – then I'm going to have to beat you over the head with my caveman stick and carry you around for a little bit."

Harper knew she shouldn't encourage him, but she couldn't stop herself from laughing. "Oh, really?"

"Really." Jared linked his fingers with hers and pressed a kiss to her knuckles before sobering. "This is your last chance to back out. If you want to turn around, now is the time to do it."

Harper calmly met his gaze. "It's going to be okay."

"I'm going to make sure of that." Jared tugged Harper in for an extended hug, making a face when Michael returned and made shooing motions to get them to separate. "Are we in your way?"

"I don't mean to be rude," Michael said. "I just don't want to lose too much of the day." He directed his team members toward the boat. "I thought we could do introductions once we set sail."

Harper nodded in agreement. "That sounds good."

"Let's do it," Jared said, pressing his hand to the small of Harper's back to prod her up the walkway. "Ludington Asylum, here we come." He said the words with a smile but couldn't muster a lot of enthusiasm, worry momentarily overtaking him.

*How did we get ourselves involved in this?*

"YOU'VE ALREADY MET Lucy and she will serve as our on-set reporter," Michael announced once everyone was seated and the boat was headed toward Ludington Asylum, one of the burly security representatives behind the wheel. "She'll want to interview everyone at various times, although she'll do her best to stay out of the action."

Lucy beamed as she glanced around at the assembled faces. "This looks like a great group."

Jared, who sat with his arm around Harper's shoulders in an effort to lend her a bit of his warmth, leaned closer so he could whisper in his girlfriend's ear. "She clearly has no idea what she's gotten herself in to."

Harper smirked but didn't speak, instead flashing a friendly smile at the woman.

"This is Trey Mitchell and Finn Barton," Michael continued, gesturing toward the two men pawing through camera equipment at the far side of the deck. "They'll be with us the entire time. And that is Steve Walker and John Hopper, who will be providing our security."

Jared flicked his eyes to the well-built men, briefly locking gazes with Steve as they sized each other up. "Do you foresee needing a lot of security?"

"No, but it's better to be safe than sorry, right?" Michael's smile was so wide it struck Jared as cheesy. "What about your group?"

Zander took over immediately and started the introductions. "I'm Zander Pritchett and this is my personal security guru Shawn Donovan. I'm a Pisces, which means I'm a bit dramatic, but you'll all grow to love me."

Jared rolled his eyes but couldn't contain his snicker. "Oh, geez."

"That loud one over there is Harper's personal bodyguard," Zander announced, jerking his thumb in Jared's direction. "He doesn't have a very good personality and he has freakishly large man nipples."

"Hey!" Jared extended a finger. "Do you want me to come over there?"

"The boat is moving," Zander replied, adopting a pragmatic tone. "That wouldn't be safe."

"Whatever," Jared muttered under his breath.

"This is Molly Parker, and in addition to having truly fabulous hair for the start of the fall season, she's also our intern," Zander continued, unbothered by Jared's attitude. "She can help in just about any situation."

Molly preened under the compliment. "Thank you."

"You're welcome." Zander turned his attention to Eric. "This is Eric Tyler. He's our equipment specialist. He monitors more than he gets involved; we don't think less of his manly abilities because of it."

"Now I'm going to come over there," Eric warned. He glared at Molly, who was belted in next to him, when she giggled. "Don't you start with me."

"And the last member of our team is the second most important," Zander said, flashing a winning smile for Harper's benefit. "She's my best friend and we started GHI together."

"I'm Harper Harlow," Harper volunteered, keeping her tone even. "I can see ... and talk ... to ghosts under the right circumstances."

For the first time since hitting the boat, the cameramen looked interested.

"You can actually see them?" Trey asked, impressed. "Most of the people we run into on stuff like this claim that they can't see anything but rather they can sense presences."

"I'm not most people."

"She's definitely not," Jared agreed, squeezing Harper's shoulder to offer her comfort. He understood she didn't like being the center of attention like this. Ultimately she would have to answer a bevy of questions – something he couldn't save her from – but that didn't mean he wouldn't do his best to make an effective shield. "While we're getting to know one another, though, I have a few suggestions for how we approach this."

Michael was clearly caught off guard by the statement. "Excuse me?"

Jared refused to let the tone get to him. "My understanding is that this island is small, but the asylum itself has a tortured history."

"Why do you think we're going?" Michael asked. "It's bound to be a wild ride."

"Which is great ... and exciting ... and I'm sure it will make terrific television," Jared said. "That doesn't mean this little trip is without risk."

"Meaning?"

"Meaning that I suggest everyone pair up with a partner," Jared replied. "No one should go anywhere alone. We don't want people getting separated."

"That's half the fun of these television shows," Finn argued. "There's nothing better than watching some idiot who thinks he's a ghost hunter – no offense, ma'am – wetting himself as he runs through the dark."

Harper bristled. "Excuse me?"

"Don't listen to him," Jared warned, scorching Finn with a dangerous look. "I honestly don't care what you do, Mr. Barton."

"Oh, please, call me Finn."

Jared ignored the ingratiating tone. "I don't care what you do. Our team will be pairing up, though."

"We will?" Eric made a face. "Oh, let me guess, that means I get Molly. How ... great."

"Like I want you as my partner," Molly groused, turning away from him. "I'd rather be eaten by ghosts on my own."

"No one is getting eaten by ghosts," Jared said. "You two are partners, though. That's just the way things worked out. If you don't like it ... well ... sorry. As for the rest, if you need to go somewhere and your partner isn't available, find someone else to go with you. No one is to go anywhere alone."

"Wow, you're really taking this seriously, huh?" Trey's expression was smarmy. "Do you actually believe your girlfriend can see ghosts?"

"I believe my girlfriend can do anything," Jared replied, refusing to back down. "I don't care what you believe. She's my partner, though, and I'll be with her the entire way."

"So ... two stars in the making," Michael interjected, rubbing his hands together as he attempted to alleviate the building tension.

"I don't want to be on camera," Jared clarified. "I will do my best to stay away from the camera. I won't be far from Harper, though. You're just going to have to get used to that."

"I'm sure everything will be fine." The strain was evident on Michael's face. "There's no reason to get riled up."

"Where Harper is concerned, I get riled up very easily." Jared rubbed his hand over Harper's shoulder. "Like I said, I'm not in charge of you guys. Our team will be following certain rules, though."

"And we're really looking forward to them," Eric muttered.

"Don't push me," Jared shot back. "It's best for everyone."

"That's easy to say when you have a partner like Harper."

Jared couldn't argue with the assessment. "Why do you think I'm saying it?"

"Okay." Harper held up her hands to cut off the argument. "We're going to stay with our partners and be careful when we hit the island. Everything is going to be okay. Once we land, get our bearings and take a look around, we'll tackle our plan of action. How does that sound?"

"It sounds great, Casper," Trey replied, his lips curving as Jared made a face. "I think this entire trip is going to be one for the ages."

## ❧ 4 ❧
### FOUR

Harper was a bundle of nerves when the island finally popped into view, digging in closer to Jared's side as she stared at the imposing building filling the skyline. She involuntarily shuddered, unable to stop herself from projecting given the horrors she knew must have occurred between the three-story building's walls.

Jared cast her a sidelong look. "Are you okay? I can make them turn this boat around if you're not."

"I'm fine." Harper made a big show of looking brave. "These guys won't turn around no matter what, by the way, but I'm fine all the same."

Jared cast a dubious look toward Michael's team. "I don't like them."

"Sometimes I think you only like me. It makes me feel special."

"I like Shawn, too," Jared teased, tightening his grip on Harper. "Oh, and Molly."

"What about Eric?"

"He's interested in you in a sexual way so, if I wasn't a cop, I would totally find a place to hide his body."

Harper giggled, Jared's lame attempt at a joke causing her to loosen up a bit. "I'm so glad you came."

Jared shifted so she had nowhere to look but into his eyes. "I am, too. There's no way I would've left you to do this alone, though."

"I wouldn't have been alone. I would've had Zander."

Jared glanced over Harper's shoulder, making a face as he watched Zander cavort with Lucy. "Yeah. That makes me feel better."

Harper snickered as she rested her head against Jared's chest. "I'm still glad you're here."

"I'll be close," Jared promised, rubbing his hands over the back of Harper's hoodie. "You make sure you don't go wandering off without me, okay?"

Harper nodded, solemn. "Believe it or not, I don't have any inclination to be away from you."

"I believe it. I've seen myself naked."

Harper laughed again, her face lighting with genuine delight. "I really do love you."

Jared cupped Harper's chin and kissed her. "Right back at you."


**THE BOAT CAPTAIN** CIRCLED THE ISLAND THREE TIMES before deciding on a place to land. There were technically two docks – although both were ravaged by time and inclement weather – and he opted for the one that looked less likely to collapse under the weight of their team.

Jared was nervous enough that he insisted people disembark two at a time, only allowing a few people on the dock at any given moment. By the time they were on the beach, they'd lost half of the afternoon.

"I think we should head inside immediately," Lucy announced. "We're going to lose the light if we don't."

"And I think we should put that off until tomorrow," Jared shot back. "I don't want to risk being caught in that building too close to dark. I think we should spend the rest of the afternoon setting up camp out here and taking a look around the island. The asylum isn't going anywhere. We can hit it first thing in the morning."

Lucy wasn't thrilled with the suggestion. "Michael, we're here to see the asylum."

"We are," Michael agreed, his expression thoughtful as he eyed

Jared. "I think Mr. Monroe has a point, though. That's a big building and we don't want to get lost inside of it. The electricity doesn't work and we need to come up with a way to mark our progress. We need time to do that."

"But ... ." Lucy's frustration was palpable.

"I agree with looking around the island first," Steve offered. "It's not very big, but it's always wise to know your surroundings."

"Oh, well, that was almost poetic," Trey deadpanned. "I'm sorry I didn't get it on camera."

"No one was talking to you," Steve snapped.

Jared and Harper exchanged a quick look. It seemed Eric and Molly weren't the only warring co-workers on the island.

"We'll set up camp," Michael stressed, drawing everyone's attention to him. "We'll build a fire and have some lunch. Then we'll take a look around the island with the light we have left before camping for the night. We'll get up first thing in the morning and tackle the asylum then."

"Fine." Lucy crossed her arms over her chest. "I still think we're missing a prime opportunity."

"And I think I prefer looking things over first," Jared said, prodding Harper to the right. "Everyone should set up their tents first. I don't think it's going to rain tonight, but it could pop up out of nowhere and we need shelter before anything else."

Harper tilted her head to the side and smiled. "You were a Boy Scout, weren't you?"

Jared shrugged. "Maybe."

"You didn't care about the polyester shirt?"

"I kind of liked it."

"Uh-huh." Harper's grin was impish. "Do you want to teach me a few of your Boy Scout tricks once we're alone tonight?"

"I've always been good at starting a fire from scratch."

"And we have the stuff to make s'mores thanks to Zander."

"I don't think we're talking about the same thing, but both sound good." Jared handed Harper the tent they would share. "Get moving, woman. As the Boy Scout, I have the most experience so I'm the boss."

Harper cocked an eyebrow. "I was a Girl Scout."

"When we need cookies, you'll be in charge."

Harper's smile slipped, causing Jared to cringe.

"I took it too far, didn't I?"

Harper nodded. "I'm going to build this tent and I don't even want your help. In fact, I might not let you sleep in it with me."

"So ... what? You'll make me bunk with Eric? That seems like cruel and unusual punishment."

"I was thinking of making you bunk with Zander. I'll bunk with Molly. Eric can bunk with Shawn."

"That's definitely cruel and unusual punishment." Jared snared Harper's belt loop before she could sashay away. "Should I start begging now or wait until you've cooled down?"

"I don't know. Maybe you should sit down and eat a cookie until I decide."

"Ugh." Jared made a disgusted sound in the back of his throat. "This is going to be a thing, isn't it?"

"You have no idea."

**HARPER WAS ANNOYED** WHEN SHE REALIZED THE TENT didn't come with instructions, but she managed to figure it out with minimal effort. By the time she was done, the blue dome gleamed majestically under the sunlight and the look she tossed Jared was one of pure haughty delight.

"Ha!"

"I stand corrected." Jared stretched in his spot on the sandy beach. "You're a master tent builder. You totally showed me."

"And?"

Jared had no idea what she expected him to say so he improvised. "And you're still the most beautiful woman in the world and not at all demanding."

"And?"

"Oh, geez." Jared leaned forward, brushing the sand off on his hands. "And I'm a schmuck?"

"Very good." Harper beamed as she leaned over to kiss him. "You're still in trouble. I just wanted that kiss as reward for my hard work. I shouldn't be punished because you're a bad boy."

"I'm going to show you exactly how bad I can be after dark," Jared teased.

"Not until after you give me a massage to reward me for all of my hard work."

"That goes without saying." Jared chuckled as he tumbled Harper into his lap, readjusting so they were both comfortable and could stare out at the peaceful lake. "The warm weather is almost gone."

"I know." Harper rested her head against Jared's chest. "I hate winter."

"Oh, come on. There has to be something you like about winter."

"The hats and boots are cute."

"This would be an instance of where you spend too much time with Zander," Jared complained. "There's a lot of fun stuff to do in the winter."

"Like what?"

"Like skiing."

"I prefer cuddling in front of a roaring fire."

"I'm good with that, too." Jared let loose with a sigh. "Do you want to look around before dinner?"

Harper shifted her gaze to the other side of the beach campsite where Shawn and Zander fussed over the food. They didn't look as if they were going to be cooking anytime soon, especially since they didn't even have a fire going yet.

"That sounds like a good idea."

Jared pushed Harper to a standing position before following, taking a moment to brush off the seat of her pants before scanning the rest of the campsite. Michael and Lucy were at the far end, their heads bent together as they discussed something. Molly watched Shawn and Zander make dinner plans, making a show of turning her back to Eric as he erected a tent. Trey and Finn checked camera equipment, seemingly in their own world. Steve and John wandered up and down the beach, making a good show of pretending they were scouting the area. Jared surmised they were largely disinterested, playing down the gig as nothing more than Hollywood nonsense. If he didn't know Harper as well as he did, he figured he would've done the same so he didn't hold it against them. That didn't mean he liked them.

"Come on, Heart." Jared linked his fingers with Harper's and tugged her toward the east side of the island. "Let's see what we can discover."

They'd only made it a few feet when Zander's voice caught up to them.

"Where are you going?"

"We're going to look around," Jared replied. "We won't be gone long."

"Make sure you're not," Zander said. "I'm making steaks and roast corn for dinner."

Jared stilled. Every time he thought he was used to Zander's rhythm and quirks, the man proved him wrong. "You're cooking steak over a campfire?"

"I am." Zander puffed out his chest. "I marinated them and everything."

"Dude, if you pull this off I'm going to take back every passive aggressive thing I ever said about you."

"What about the aggressive ones?"

"Probably not, but I'll feel bad about them." Jared smiled as he led Harper away from the group. Since the sun was still relatively high in the sky – although nights came much earlier in Michigan this time of year – he wasn't worried about being too far away from the group as long as the illumination lasted. After that, though, he had every intention of keeping close to camp. He wasn't psychic. He couldn't see or talk to ghosts. He could sense the feeling of dread seeping out from the asylum, though. It set his teeth on edge.

The island was small, more than fifty percent of it made up of beach. The asylum sat in the middle of the landmass, overgrown weeds and bushes crowding the first-floor windows. The second floor boasted a beautiful stained-glass window that remained mostly intact – except for a few errant panels that had fallen over the years – but the building itself was in terrible condition.

"I'm almost afraid to look inside," Jared noted as they walked. "If it's this bad outside, what do you think it has inside?"

"Ghosts."

"Have you seen any?"

"Well ... no," Harper hedged. "I feel them, though. I'm sure that sounds unbelievable, but I feel them. They're watching us."

"Nothing you do seems unbelievable. Miraculous would be a better word."

"Are you still sucking up?"

"Yes, but I wasn't even thinking about that," Jared replied. "I believe whatever you say. You're ... magical."

Harper's smile was rueful. "Now you're definitely sucking up."

"It's not considered sucking up if it's true." Jared swung their arms, enjoying the way their melded shadows looked thanks to the setting sun. "What do you think about the people on the island with us?"

"I think that the security guys are jerks."

"I think that anyone who meets them believes that."

"You're obviously much smarter and stronger."

"Now who is sucking up?" Jared challenged.

"Just because it's true that doesn't mean it's sucking up."

"Ha, ha." Jared flicked Harper's ear and exhaled heavily, the shadow of the asylum hitting him just right and blocking out the sun. "What about Michael? What do you think about him?"

"He's nowhere near as handsome as you."

"I don't need my ego bolstered. I really want to know what you think."

"I think he's worried about your presence on the island," Harper replied, opting for honesty. "He's afraid you'll use your influence to affect the way I react to the ghosts."

"Meaning?"

"He doesn't think I'm the real deal, which I'm fine with."

"You're not fine with it," Jared countered. "That's okay, though. I would be upset if I were in your shoes as well."

"I'm not upset. I'm used to it."

"You are used to it – which is a travesty of justice – but you're also upset," Jared said. "It's okay. I'm not going to judge you."

"He's a big weenie and he thinks he's fooling me," Harper conceded, causing Jared to bark out a delighted laugh. "He's fooling Zander and Molly, though. Eric is more standoffish – and clearly has something else on his mind revolving around Molly that I can't quite wrap my head around – so he isn't snowed yet."

"I don't think Zander is snowed as much as he's got stars in his eyes," Jared corrected. "If push comes to shove, which I don't foresee happening, he will take your side. The guy drives me nuts, but he's loyal to you. He'll always take your side."

"He will." Harper bobbed her head. "The wild cards are the cameramen. I can't quite get a firm reading on either of them. They seem ... engaged on one level and dubious on another. I'm not sure how to describe it."

"I know what you're saying," Jared said. "I'm guessing these guys very rarely work with the real deal, or visit locations that are actually haunted. They probably think they're in for a good show and nothing else."

"I'm worried that they *are* going to be in for a good show," Harper admitted. "I think tomorrow is going to be very, very interesting."

"Then you'd better stay very, very close to me."

Harper laughed as Jared caught her around the waist and dipped her low. They'd made a complete circle of the island – it was so small there was literally nowhere to hide except inside of the building – and they were out in the open when Jared lavishly kissed her.

"Knock that off," Zander called out. "You're going to give me indigestion before I even start eating."

"Shut up," Jared shot back, glaring over his shoulder. He didn't pay attention as Harper extricated herself and dropped to one knee close to the shoreline. "My steak better be delicious, by the way, or I'm totally going passive aggressive with you for the rest of the night."

"Your steak will be delicious, but I'm not doing it for you," Zander said. "I'm doing it for the sake of the steak."

"Oh, well ... that sounds delightful." Jared slid his eyes to Harper, frowning when he realized she'd missed the bulk of the conversation. "What are you looking at?"

Harper held up something, gold glinting under the sunlight. "I found it."

Jared snagged the gold bracelet from her and flipped it over so he could read the faded lettering on the name bar. "I wonder who Julie is."

"Do you think it's been out here since the seventies?"

"No, it wouldn't be in this good of shape," Jared replied, peering closer. "I don't think it's been out here more than a few days, maybe a few weeks at the most."

"How did it get here?"

Jared shrugged. "I'm guessing this island makes a great party place for teenagers," Jared replied. "Think about it. There are a lot of kids who can get to this location without getting hassled by adults. They probably party out here all summer."

Harper flicked her eyes to the asylum. "Do you think they go inside?"

"I think that when you get alcohol in teenagers that common sense goes out the window." Jared slipped the bracelet into his pocket before grabbing Harper's hand and giving it a squeeze. "Don't worry about it, Heart. Nobody has gone missing in recent weeks, at least to my knowledge. I'm sure it's fine."

Harper wasn't convinced. "Then why is the bracelet still here?"

"Because it's broken and someone clearly lost it. It's real gold, but that doesn't mean it's valuable."

"Okay, but ... ."

"No buts." Jared pressed his finger to Harper's lips to quiet her. "There's no reason to get worked up ... at least not until tomorrow morning when we step into the belly of the beast. Until then, we can enjoy ourselves.

"Come on," he continued. "Zander is cooking steak over a campfire, I'm going to give you a romantic massage, and we're in a tent so when I make a move after dark everyone is going to hear us and think I'm the ultimate stud. What's not to love?"

Harper was reluctant to let it go, but she didn't have a lot of options so she did just that. "I'm kind of curious about the steak myself."

"I'm just glad we brought cookies in case it's a disaster."

Harper's smile faded. "Do you really want to go back to the cookies?"

"Only if it means I can grovel some more."

"I'm always open to that."

## FIVE

"**I**'m officially in love with you."

Harper pressed her lips together to keep from laughing when she realized Jared was talking to Zander while collecting paper plates in a garbage bag after dinner. He'd spent the entire meal "oohing" and "aahing" over the food, making small yummy noises that tickled Harper and caused Zander to preen. She loved it when the two most important men in her life got along.

"Aw, you're sweet." Zander patted Jared's cheek before sliding his empty plate in the bag. "I'm spoken for, though."

"He is," Shawn agreed, although his eyes lit with mirth. "I understand the love, though. That was a terrific meal, Zander."

"It was," Harper agreed, her eyes narrowing when Jared didn't move to return to her. "And I'm starting to feel neglected," she added pointedly.

"Sorry." Jared shook his head, giving the campground a once over before handing the bag to John. "You're going to want to make sure that's put somewhere scavengers can't get to it."

John arched an eyebrow as he accepted the bag. "Do you think the island has bears or something? Perhaps it will be like *Lost*."

"No, but that doesn't mean there aren't rats," Jared replied, maintaining a thin veneer of calm. "Do you want to wake up to rats in our camp?"

"I certainly don't," Zander said, grinning when Jared shot him an appreciative look.

Jared returned his weighted gaze to John and held it there for several beats. "I'm not going to be happy if we're invaded by rats."

"Are you ever happy?" John challenged. "From what I can tell, nothing, but the blonde makes you happy."

The observation didn't bother Jared in the least. "She's what makes me happiest. I would be lying if I said I wasn't happy with the fact that Zander just cooked a gourmet steak over a campfire, though."

"Okay, okay." Michael clapped his hands to get everyone's attention. He was a smart man and he hadn't missed the underlying tension spilling out between the two groups all afternoon. "I thought we would spend some time going over the history of the asylum tonight – make sure everyone is prepared for what might be inside – and then go to bed early."

Jared spared one more dark look for John before returning to Harper, positioning himself so he sat behind her – Harper protected with her back against his chest and a shared blanket spread over them as he wrapped his arms around her and rested his chin on her shoulder – and got comfortable next to the fire.

"I think that's a good idea." Harper shifted, nervous. "I'm guessing most everyone doesn't know the history of this place."

"I looked it up after Zander mentioned going," Shawn volunteered. "It sounds as if a lot of bad things happened out here."

"That seems to be the general consensus," Harper agreed.

"We did a lot of research on the place when we were kids," Zander explained. "Harper really wanted to come see it, but Uncle Mel wouldn't loan us his boat ... or bring us here himself. He said it was a bad idea."

Since Mel Kelsey also happened to be his partner, Jared snickered as he snuggled closer to Harper. Even though it was terribly cold, their camping spot on the beach offered little shelter other than the tents and Jared worried Harper would come down with a chill. "That sounds just like him. Why didn't you take your dad's boat, Heart?"

Harper shrugged. "He didn't think it was a good idea either and strictly forbade us to come out here."

"Yes, and you always do what your father wants."

"Even then I knew it was probably a bad idea to come out here," Harper said, her eyes flicking to the asylum's ominous façade. It was dark enough that the building appeared to loom into the sky, a monstrous shadow stalking them before sleep. "I was curious and afraid, if that makes sense."

"But you could see ghosts then, right?" Steve asked, his expression neutral.

"I could."

"And how long have you been able to see ghosts?" Steve was either curious or trying to gather information to give himself a good laugh once he was away from everyone for the night. Jared couldn't decide which. He definitely didn't like the man's attitude, though.

"Since I was a kid," Harper replied. She'd been expecting questions. Now was hardly the time to run from them. "My grandfather came to say goodbye to me the night he died. I was a child at the time. I didn't understand what he was saying, until my parents came into my bedroom and told me that he'd passed away during the night."

"Oh, wow," Lucy enthused, leaning forward. "Did he tell you any secrets? Maybe ... did he tell you where he buried some money?"

Harper wrinkled her nose. "My grandfather wasn't big on hiding money."

"So what did he tell you?" Finn asked, legitimately curious. "He must've had something on his mind."

"He did." Harper bobbed her head. "He told me he loved me."

"Oh, that's kind of ... a letdown." Trey made a face. "That's not much of a ghost story."

"I happen to like it," Jared gritted out. It took everything he had not to hop over the fire and smash his fist into Trey's face. "If you don't like it, you could do the polite thing and shut your hole."

Zander chuckled, the sound filling the night air with a sense of ease that wasn't present only seconds before. "You might want to be careful there, Trey," he warned. "We're all loyal to Harper. We know what she can do. It's best not to underestimate her."

"Did I say I was underestimating her?" Trey challenged.

"No, but Jared has a keen nose for uncovering these things and his sense of humor tends to fly out the window when people attack Harper," Zander replied. "For the record, my sense of humor doesn't last long under those circumstances either."

Trey wasn't about to back down. "Is that supposed to frighten me? Are you guys going to beat me up?"

"No, but I will cut you off from our food supply." Zander was pragmatic at the oddest of times. "If you want to keep it up, I'll cook for our group and you can eat … what is it? Hot dogs and potato chips, I believe you said. You can eat that with your people."

"Hey, I don't want to be cut off from the food," Finn protested.

"Then tell your friend to shut his mouth," Jared snapped.

"Yes, because if one of you is rude to Harper, then I'm going to assume that all of you feel the same way." Zander's smile was serene, but there was a gleam in his eyes. He was angry and refused to hide it. "Tomorrow we're having omelets and hash browns for breakfast. I believe Michael brought cold Pop-Tarts for you."

Finn's mouth dropped open, abject horror flashing across his face. "That's just mean."

"That's how I roll."

Michael cleared his throat in an effort to get back on track. "I believe we can all agree that getting along is our top priority."

"I thought our top priority was seeing ghosts?" Finn challenged, doing his best to focus everyone's attention in Michael's direction. The only two who didn't follow his lead were Trey and Jared, who openly glared at one another across the fire.

"That, too," Michael conceded, a small smile playing at the corner of his lips. "As for the asylum itself, how much of the history are you familiar with, Harper?"

Harper linked her fingers with Jared's under the blanket and forced herself to remain calm. "I've kept up on all of the asylum's history."

"Why don't you share a bit of it with us?" Michael suggested.

"Okay, well … ." Harper broke off, licking her lips. She was nervous about being the center of attention given the makeup of the group, but she refused to back down from a challenge.

"It's okay, Heart." Jared kissed her cheek. "I want to hear all about it, too."

"John Jacob Bennett was a doctor at one of the big Detroit hospitals in the 1940s," Harper started, internally thankful Jared insisted on sharing his warmth with her for story hour. "He was young then and he had an interest in mental health treatment.

"You have to remember that mental health treatment back then isn't what it is now," she continued. "Now we tend to use drugs more than anything else. Then they used, well, I'm not sure torture is the politically correct term, but it's certainly apt. A lot of the treatments back then – lobotomies, insulin-induced comas, electroshock therapy, and even malaria – aren't things we would consider allowing today."

"Malaria?" Trey sat in the spot next to Steve, interested despite himself. "How did that work?"

"They basically introduced inoculated malaria into a person's bloodstream and thought the malaria-induced fever would knock the crazy out of people," Harper explained.

"You have got to be kidding." Finn made a face. "That sounds ... barbaric."

"We've made huge advancements in mental health treatment over the course of the past sixty years, but these things take time," Harper explained. "In the 1950s, there was a push to stop putting people in asylums and sanitariums as a way of treatment but before then ... well ... there was very little oversight."

"You mentioned that the other night," Jared said, shifting so he could rest his back against his pack and keep both of them comfortable. "The way you phrased it made me believe that no one ever came out here to check and see what was being done with the patients."

"Right. I'm getting ahead of myself." Harper shook her head as she tried to remember where she was in the story. "So John Jacob Bennett came from a rich family. His grandfather was a surgeon. So was his father. Back then that was a lucrative profession and the family owned one of those big mansions in Grosse Pointe.

"Bennett wasn't as skilled as his father and grandfather and couldn't pass the surgical boards so he made mental health his focus," she continued. "He wanted to open a sanitarium on Belle Isle but was turned down. The city officials didn't think that was a good idea.

"Bennett got his chance in the 1930s when a local woman apparently lost it and killed her four children and husband." Harper was lost in her story. "The woman was clearly delusional, ranting and raving about voices telling her to do it. She didn't believe her family was dead and thought the police were keeping them from her. She clearly wasn't fit to stand trial, so there was a public debate about what to do with her."

"And that's when Bennett stepped in?" Jared prodded.

"Basically, yes. Bennett suggested a lockdown facility and residents weren't happy with the idea of an institution like that being housed in a residential neighborhood. He suggested an island and ... voila. They found this island."

"Who funded the institution?" Trey asked. "This place had to have cost money."

"It certainly did," Harper confirmed. "It wasn't an easy sell. Ultimately, in exchange for making him the chief, the Bennett family funded construction and arranged to provide for transportation. Patients were only ferried in once a week, the same as supplies, and otherwise it was run without much interference."

"It was a state hospital, though, right?" Eric asked.

"It was, and technically it fell under state regulations and oversight, but given the location, it's my understanding that no one ever bothered to check on the institution because the logistics associated with conducting spot inspections were simply too difficult."

"That was convenient for Bennett, huh?" Lucy stretched out her long legs, giving the men around the campfire an enticing view. "He could do whatever he wanted."

"There's not a lot known about the inner workings of the asylum during his tenure," Harper explained. "The files were listed as 'incomplete' when the state came in and took over operations."

"You said a lot of the patients were never accounted for," Jared prodded. "You also said no bodies were discovered on the island. It's too small for them to have been burying a bunch of bodies out here without anyone noticing."

"Yeah, but they had a crematorium for at least some of that time," Zander volunteered.

Harper stilled, her eyes locking with Zander's. "Holy crap. I forgot all about that."

"I don't remember seeing mention of a crematorium," Michael said, reaching for the stack of files he always carried. "Wouldn't that be on the building plans?"

"They had a crematorium," Harper supplied. "I forgot about it until Zander mentioned it, but it was at the back of the building. I saw the spot where the stack used to be when Jared and I were walking. I don't think my mind put that together until Zander reminded me of that story."

"You saw a fallen smokestack?" Jared tilted his head down. "I didn't see that."

"The big stack of bricks on the back of the building. That used to be the crematorium stack. I believe the actual crematorium was in the basement and the stack came through the ground and vented on that side."

"How do you know the crematorium was real?" Jared asked.

"I saw photos and it was in some of the library files I read when I was a kid," Harper replied. "It was real. That was mentioned – very briefly, mind you – in some of the older news stories about the asylum when it was shut down. They never overtly said that bodies were burned on the premises to cover up misdeeds, but if you read between the lines I think it was clear that law enforcement officials believed that even if they could never prove it."

"That would make sense," Michael mused. "I've read a lot of the files and the police were convinced that Bennett was killing patients. They simply didn't know if it was through malpractice or on purpose."

"It could've been a mixture of both," Harper said. "No matter what, when we go inside that building tomorrow, there are bound to be a lot of displaced spirits running around. Because of the island's isolation factor, that means they could be more active than normal."

Lucy leaned forward, her interest piqued. "What does that mean?"

"It means that I expect a lot of activity tomorrow," Harper replied. "I think the asylum was a very unhappy place and when terrible things happen in one location – like this one – then it leaves a mark."

"Ghosts?" Trey's lips quirked.

Harper didn't hesitate when answering. "Most definitely."

"Will you talk to them?"

"I guess we'll have to see." Harper moved to stand, Jared helping her. "I'm really tired so I'm going to bed. I'll see you guys in the morning."

"I'll be right there," Jared called out, his eyes keen as he watched her go. He waited until he was sure she was out of earshot before speaking again. "I've about had it with the snide remarks."

Michael balked. "I've been nothing but respectful."

"You've been something else entirely," Jared countered. "That's not the point." He planted his gaze on Trey. "If you keep going after her, I'm going to go after you."

"And he's a police officer so he can make it hurt," Zander added.

"I can," Jared agreed. "I'm only going to put up with so much."

"What about your girlfriend?" Trey asked. "How much is she going to put up with?"

"If you push me, you'll find out." Jared stared down Trey for a long beat before shaking his head. "I'm going to bed. Try to keep it down if you're going to stay up."

"I'm going to make s'mores and tell ghost stories," Zander said. "Finn actually spent a couple of years growing up on the west side of the city and we're going to compare notes because he can't really remember a lot about his time here. Wait ... Harper didn't get her s'more."

"Bring her one as a surprise," Jared suggested, smiling. "I think she'll like it."

"Aren't you guys going to be doing the dirty?" Zander queried. "There's no door for me to knock on."

"I'll wait until you deliver the s'more."

"Okay." Zander's smile was bright. "Take care of our girl. She looks ... tired."

"She does," Jared agreed, worry niggling the back of his brain. "We're going to take care of her together."

"Does that mean you want me to sleep with you guys?"

Jared scowled. "For the record, I never want that."

"I promise not to make fun of your big nipples."

Jared's expression turned sour. "Even when I like you there are times I want to punch you. I'm not sure how you manage it."

"It's a gift."

"Maybe you should return it."

## 6

## SIX

Harper's sleep was restless, her mind littered with a myriad of terrible images. She was certain her subconscious created the issues rather than her abilities suddenly expanding so she could see the past, but she remained unsettled when Zander pressed a mug of coffee into her hand by the campfire the next morning.

"What do you want in your omelet, Harp?"

"What?" Harper, lost in her own head, jerked her chin up and found Zander staring at her. "What did you say?"

"I asked what you want in your omelet."

"Oh, well ... ." Harper's stomach writhed with nerves at the prospect of eating. "I think I'll just stick with coffee this morning."

"No, you won't," Jared argued, appearing at her side. "You need to eat. It's going to be a long day and you need fuel."

"I don't feel all that well." Harper pressed a hand to her stomach. "Maybe in a little bit I will feel better."

"In an hour we're going to be inside the asylum," Michael pointed out. "Now is the time to eat."

"And you're eating," Jared added. "You need to at least try."

Harper blew out a sigh as she bundled the black hoodie she wore more tightly around her. "Fine. Just mushrooms and cheese."

"That doesn't sound like much of an omelet," Zander complained.

"I'm afraid if you add anything else I'll hurl." She forced a smile. "And no one wants that. If I hurl, I won't get any kisses."

"Yes, you will." Jared stroked the back of her head. "I brought gum."

"Oh, nice." Zander winked at Jared, their gazes briefly locking and something unsaid passing between them. Zander broke the eye contact first and turned to the rest of the group. "I'm taking orders."

"I want whatever you have," Trey said, pouring a mug of coffee as he scanned Harper's profile. "I'm not picky."

"You get Pop-Tarts," Zander shot back. "I don't like you much after last night."

"Aw, come on." Trey made a sheepish face. "I didn't mean to upset you or anything. I was just joking around."

"Perhaps you should read some topical books on humor," Zander suggested. "It doesn't matter, though. No omelet for you. If you adjust your attitude, I might allow you to have some of the homemade fried chicken I'm making for dinner tonight."

"Oh, come on." Jared was dumbfounded. "How are you going to make fried chicken out here?"

"I'm not sure you should get an omelet either," Zander chirped. "If you doubt my abilities after last night ... ."

"Make him an omelet," Shawn prodded. "He needs his strength, too."

Zander let loose with a long-suffering sigh. "Fine."

Jared shot Shawn a thumbs-up before turning his attention to Michael. "What's the plan for this morning?"

Michael's expression was blank. "What do you mean? We're going into the asylum."

Jared bit back his temper. "I know that. Do you have an internal map or anything?"

"Oh, yeah." Michael brightened as he dug in his files, returning with a building map. "Here it is."

Jared took the map as he sat next to Harper, pressing his leg against hers in a show of solidarity. She was unnaturally quiet – something he didn't like – and he wanted to make sure she didn't feel abandoned or alone for the duration of their stay.

"So we're going in here." Jared rested the map on his knees, ignoring the irritation that bubbled up when John and Steve meandered over to look over his shoulder. "It seems the first room is a lobby of sorts. The kitchen and dining facilities look to be off to the right – and I'm sure they're picturesque after decades of abandonment – and there's another big room over here."

Harper followed Jared's finger as he traced the map. "That's the common room."

Jared cocked an eyebrow. "How do you know that?"

"I've looked over the internal maps numerous times." Harper collected the map. "The main floor is essentially kitchen and dining areas and the common room. There's also a set of classrooms toward the back, but I'm not sure how much learning ever got done out here."

"Okay." Jared was happy she decided to engage in the conversation. "You said the crematorium was in the basement but suggested it was shut down at one point." He narrowed his eyes as he flipped pages. "That's this map. Do you know what all of these little rooms were for?"

Harper nodded, her expression morose. "They were treatment rooms."

Jared moved his hands to the back of Harper's neck, finding the muscles tight and bunched. She was a huge bundle of coiled energy and he worried she would blow before it was all said and done. "We won't go into those."

"Hey!" Michael made a disgusted sound in the back of his throat. "We're definitely going in those rooms. Do you have any idea how creepy the footage from those rooms will be?"

"I don't care what you do," Jared fired back. "You can do whatever you want. If Harper doesn't want to go to any particular spots, she doesn't have to. If you try to make her – or manipulate her, for that matter – I will shut this down."

"We have signed contracts."

"And I'm a police officer who can deem this excursion unsafe for everyone." Jared narrowed his eyes to dangerous slits. "Don't push me."

"You keep saying that, man," Trey noted. "I'm confused. Are we supposed to be afraid of you?"

"And no fried chicken for you either," Zander muttered, causing Trey to scowl.

"I take it back," Trey muttered, his expression matching Harper's. "I was just joking."

"I wasn't," Jared said. "Harper is an adult and can do whatever she wants. I'm not her keeper. If I feel that a room is unsafe – and this entire building could very well be unsafe – then I will step in. I'm not risking her for anything."

"No one wants that," Michael said hurriedly. "We all want this to be a safe trip."

Jared wasn't so sure. "We'll hit the main floor this morning and then discuss future plans over lunch. I want Harper to get a feeling for the building before we make any big decisions."

Michael didn't look happy with the announcement, but he didn't put up a fight. "That sounds like a workable plan."

"Great." Jared shifted to find Harper staring at the basement plans. "What is it, Heart?"

"I don't know," Harper replied after a beat. "Everything just feels ... heavy."

"Yeah? If things get too heavy, I will place a call and get Mel out here to collect us," Jared said. "Don't be afraid to put a stop to this if it gets to be too much."

For the first time since waking up, Harper flashed a genuine grin. "That won't make Mel happy."

"I don't care."

"I don't either," Zander said. "I'm his favorite nephew. He has to ride to the rescue if we need it. It's in the Good Uncle Handbook."

"No one is going to need a rescue," Michael argued. "It's a simple ghost shoot. We've done hundreds of these before."

"You've never done one like this before," Harper said. "I guarantee that."

**HARPER CHOKED DOWN** THE BULK OF HER BREAKFAST,

actually feeling better for the effort once Jared gathered her plate. She excused herself for a quick bathroom break with Molly, moving to a spot behind some sad-looking trees before washing her hands in the lake and focusing her full attention on the asylum.

It didn't take everyone long to collect themselves, and by the time they were moving in that direction Harper had managed to tuck away the bulk of her fear. She was excited to see inside of the structure – it was something she wished for a long time ago and it was finally coming to fruition, after all – but she remained a bit nervous.

Jared stood close, constantly finding a reason to touch her in an effort to offer small bouts of reassurance. Michael had official permission to be on the island from the state and the key he dug from his pocket and pointed toward the lock looked fresh and new.

"Someone has been out here," Jared noted, eying the lock with some interest. "That chain and lock are new."

"I believe they come out once a season to check on the property," Michael explained. "When I first broached the subject of filming out here they weren't happy with the suggestion. They changed their minds after a little bit, though, and allowed scouting and one weekend's worth of filming. I think they're hoping they might be able to sell the island."

"Sell it?" Eric made a face as he tilted his head and took in the imposing façade. "Why would anyone want this island?"

"They could tear down the asylum," Molly suggested, sticking close to Eric despite the fact that they appeared to barely be on speaking terms. "They could put something else out here."

"Like what?"

"They could put a refreshment stand or something out here," Zander offered. "I mean, think about it. This lake is full of boaters in the summer. It could be a destination for them if they want to drop anchor and enjoy the island."

"That's a fun idea," Shawn enthused. "Someone who likes isolation might be interested in buying a house out here, too. It's only a ten-minute boat ride from the Harsens Island dock."

"You couldn't pay me to live out here," Jared said, flicking his eyes to Michael when he heard the lock snick.

"I've got it," Michael crowed. "It's open."

"Congratulations," Steve said dryly. "Perhaps you'll get a trophy when you get back home."

Michael ignored the sarcasm. "Is everybody ready? Cameras ready?"

"We're ready," Finn said, hoisting his camera to his shoulder. "You should open the doors and let us get a couple of shots before anyone goes inside."

"Good idea."

Harper moved out of the way, her eyes keen as Michael dramatically threw open the door. Finn and Trey immediately stepped up to film, their movements slow and deliberate. For her part, Harper leaned forward in an attempt to see through the murk. The building was so dark that it was virtually impossible to see more than a few feet inside, though.

"I was afraid of this," Michael lamented after a beat. "I brought flashlights just in case." He bent over and dug in the duffel bag at his feet. "I have one for everyone and included a few extras, too. I also have a ton of batteries, so don't be afraid to use them."

Harper wordlessly accepted a flashlight, immediately flicking it on. She felt a bit silly at the relief coursing through her – it was a simple flashlight, after all – but she kept the emotion to herself.

"Are we ready to go in?" Michael looked beyond excited. "You should go first, Harper. You're the star."

Harper didn't feel like much of a star, but she squeezed Jared's hand before moving to the opening. He immediately started to follow, but Trey stilled him with a shake of his head.

"If you don't want to be on camera then you can't crowd her," Trey chastised. "Make a decision."

Jared frowned. "Listen ... ."

"It's fine," Harper said hurriedly, placing her hand on Jared's arm. "Just stay close. I won't be far away."

"I'll definitely stay close," Jared muttered, although he was grateful when Zander immediately moved to Harper's side so he could walk through the door with her. Of course, Zander was wearing a man purse – something he unveiled right after breakfast – and it supposedly contained numerous items that might come in handy during their search. Jared had a feeling Zander was going to regret wearing the purse on camera, but it was hardly a big concern for the distracted police officer.

Shawn shifted so he walked next to Jared. "He'll take care of her. Plus, well, he wants to be on camera. It's the best of both worlds."

Jared remained dubious. "What about you? Don't you want to be on camera?"

"Not even remotely," Shawn replied. "This whole thing freaks me out."

Jared was loath to admit it, but he felt the same way. "I can't wait until this weekend is over. I'm going to spend an entire day in bed with Harper – no visitors allowed – and just freaking relax."

"I'm sure we can make that happen." Shawn offered a sallow smile, his kind heart coming out to play. "She's going to be okay. I can see that you're worried but ... she's going to be okay."

Jared fervently wanted to believe that. "I'll make sure she is."

"You will."

The duo lapsed into companionable silence as they slid into the asylum. The building, although old, sagging, and missing windows, felt oppressive and closed in.

"Do you feel that?" Lucy whispered. "I think we're surrounded by ghosts." She seemed the excitable sort, so Jared brushed off her reaction until he scanned Harper's face. She was whiter than any ghost he'd ever imagined.

"Heart." Jared stepped forward, ignoring the dirty look Trey shot in his direction. "Are you okay?"

Harper pressed her lips together and nodded, her eyes wide as they bounced to every corner of the room. "I saw photographs from when it was in operation," she whispered. "It's the same. I mean, it's dirty, gross, and there's probably something creepy and crawly living in here, but otherwise it's still the same. It's as if time hasn't touched this building."

Jared gently slipped a strand of Harper's hair behind her ear. "Where do you want to go first?" He was determined to make sure she had control of the situation, whether Michael and his crew liked it or not.

"I think we should go to the basement," Michael said.

"I wasn't talking to you," Jared growled. "And that's not happening. We've already talked about it."

"We don't want to get to the big stuff right away," Zander added, tightening his grip on his man purse. His expression was bright, but his eyes flashed with trepidation. "Don't we want to build up to the big stuff?"

"He has a point," Lucy said. "We should start small and build bigger."

"That means we need to stick to this floor until after lunch," Jared stressed. "I want to make sure this building is safe – er, at least mildly safe – before we consider going up or down."

"I agree with him," Steve added. "This building is old and ... aside from being unsanitary, we need to check floorboards and stairs before anyone moves across them."

"Fine." Michael said the words, but he didn't appear happy. "Whatever you want, Harper."

Harper ignored the chilly cast of his tone and fixed her eyes to the left. "The common room is over there. If you look closely, you can see some natural light spilling in. I'm pretty sure those are the broken-out windows we saw during our walk yesterday."

"Which means there's probably critters living in there," Trey said.

"There's also natural light and it should look good for the cameras," Harper noted. "We're going to look in multiple rooms. There's no reason we can't start there."

"None that I can see," Jared agreed, kissing her cheek before taking a step back. "Lead the way, Heart."

"Yeah, *Heart*," Trey mimicked.

"No fresh cookies for you either," Zander hissed, linking his arm with Harper's as they walked ahead.

Harper was glad for the contact, and her eyes were busy as they walked toward the expansive doorway. Even though the floor felt solid despite years of abandonment, she was careful with each step. She didn't want to accidentally fall through some errant hole in the floor – that was a reoccurring nightmare she suffered from as a kid – and by the time they hit the large wooden doors that separated the main foyer from the common room she was entranced with the ornate setting.

"The woodwork is very expensive," Harper said, running her hand over the doorframe. "They went top of the line when they built this place."

"It's too bad it was all for naught," Michael said.

"Yeah, but it left a pretty mark behind."

Zander released Harper's arm at Finn's silent prodding and took a step back, moving closer to Shawn, so the cameraman could get a good shot of his best friend. Harper, lost in her own little world, didn't notice as she stepped over the threshold. She was too busy gazing at the faded wallpaper and overbearing light fixtures.

"They must have spent thousands of dollars on the chandeliers alone," Harper mused. She didn't realize she was significantly ahead of the rest of the group because she was too caught up in the ambiance. "This clearly wasn't a normal state hospital."

Jared was almost to the door before he realized how far Harper had gotten ahead of them. "Heart ... ." He didn't get a chance to finish, because at that exact moment a chilly blast of air whooshed through the room – despite the fact that it couldn't have originated from the direction it came given the walls standing in the way – and blew back the group members.

Jared fought against the wind, his only thought of getting to Harper. If he pushed through, he thought he would be by her side within seconds.

That didn't happen, though, because the wind was so strong it managed to blow shut the door, separating a surprised Harper from the rest of the group. The wind died as quickly as it stirred, and all that was left was silence ... and fear.

"Harper!"

## 7

# SEVEN

Jared clawed at the door, twisting the handle and growling in frustration when it broke off in his hand.

"Harper!" He beat on the door, desperate.

"Chill out." Steve cast Jared a wary look as he used his hip to nudge the panicked police detective to the side. "It's probably just stuck."

"That doesn't make me feel any better." Jared viciously kicked the door before giving Steve room to operate. "Get it open."

"Okay." Steve exchanged an amused look with John, clearly enjoying himself, and pressed on the solid panel. "Hmm. This thing is freaking oak. I can't believe it's in this good of condition given how long it's been exposed to ... just about everything ... out here."

"Yes, we can all marvel at the craftsmanship later," Jared barked. "Open it!"

"Harper?" Zander moved to the hinges and tried to peer through the small opening between the door and the jamb. It was too dark to see anything, but that didn't stop him from trying. "Answer us right now, Harp."

"I'm okay."

Jared almost collapsed with relief when he heard her voice, taking a moment to collect himself before speaking. "What happened?"

"I'm not sure." Harper's voice sounded small, as if it was coming from very far away. "I felt some wind, but it didn't seem to be coming through the open windows. They're too high up for that. Then the door slammed shut."

"Are you okay?"

"I'm okay."

"We're trying to get the door open, but we're going to need some tools," Steve supplied. "You need to hold on for a few minutes. You're not going to fall apart, are you?"

"I think I'll survive," Harper said dryly, and Jared almost smiled because he could picture the dirty look on her face.

"Stay close to the door, Heart," Jared ordered. "Don't go wandering around."

"There's nothing in here," Harper argued. "I won't go far but ... I'm going to look."

"Don't you dare."

"Just for a second."

"Son of a ... ." Jared mimed strangling an invisible person – much to Steve's amusement – and scowled. "Sometimes I think she's trying to kill me."

"She's a woman," Steve said pragmatically. "They all feel like that."

"No, she's special."

Steve pursed his lips, amused. "I never would've guessed that you think she's special. I guess those hearts floating around your head whenever you look at her are just a figment of my imagination, huh?"

"Get this door open," Jared barked, refusing to be drawn into an argument. "I'm going outside and working my way around the building from there. I might be able to break out one of the windows."

"Um, I'm not okay with that," Michael said. "We promised not to do any damage. We signed a contract."

"The entire building is damaged," Jared pointed out. "How will they know what we did and what was already done?"

"He has a point," Steve said. "Don't go alone, though."

Jared rolled his eyes. "I'm perfectly capable of taking care of myself."

"It's your rule," Steve reminded him. "I thought it was ridiculous when you insisted on it but ... don't go alone."

Jared made an odd whimpering sound in the back of his throat before turning his attention to Shawn. "Do you want to come with me?"

Shawn nodded without hesitation. "Absolutely." He stopped long enough to place a hand on Zander's arm. "Stay with Eric and Molly."

Zander nodded, distracted. "Get her. I'll be here if we manage to get the door open before you do."

Jared nodded, understanding. "Thanks. We won't be gone long."

**HARPER DID HER** BEST TO IGNORE THE VOICES ON THE OTHER side of the door. She knew Jared was probably close to a stroke, but there was nothing she could do about it at present so she pushed it out of her mind.

She utilized small steps as she explored the room. It was huge – running the entire length of the east side of the structure – but it only appeared to have one door.

"That's odd," Harper murmured, slowly tracking her flashlight over the wall to make sure she didn't miss an exit. The doorframe was wide, which was typical of the time period's designers, but a room this size could've easily housed a hundred patients at a time. Harper very much doubted it ever did, but the lack of emergency exits was curious.

A hint of movement near the ceiling caught Harper's attention, but when she pointed her light in that direction the only thing she found was spider webs ... and what looked to be mildew.

"I'm guessing the maids have been busy."

Harper continued her trek, keeping one ear on the door should it open, but the bulk of her attention on the furnishings. Odd lumps of fabric – what looked to have been couches at one time – littered the walls. The fabric was filthy and damp, although Harper couldn't find a source for the water.

"Maybe it leaks when it rains."

Harper felt silly talking to herself, but hearing something – anything really – was better than letting her fear take hold. She shuffled to the center of the room, pointing the light at the walls and discarded items as she turned in a circle. Once. Twice. It was almost mesmerizing.

"It's as if one day this place was fully functional and the next it wasn't," she mused, shaking her head. "When it closed, it must've happened fast."

"It did."

Harper gasped at the new voice, swiveling quickly. She almost lost hold of the flashlight but barely managed to hang on, and by the time she grappled with it and focused on the ethereal being floating a few feet away, she felt like an idiot. Had the ghost been aggressive, Harper could've been seriously hurt in the time it took her to collect her wits. Thankfully for Harper, the ghostly woman watching her with unveiled interest didn't look to be dangerous.

"Sorry. You took me by surprise." Harper forced a smile. "Do you live here?"

The woman nodded, her lips curving. She was pretty, in a sickly sort of way, of course. She looked a bit malnourished and as if she didn't get enough vitamin D when she was alive. She wore a tattered nightgown, the fabric fraying at the bottom hem and arms, and an unreadable expression. She appeared relatively friendly, though, which Harper thought was probably a good thing given the situation.

"I do."

"How ... um ... long have you lived here?"

The woman's smile was kind. "Longer, I would guess, then you've been alive."

Harper remembered her manners quickly, internally chastising herself for forgetting the first thing she learned when dealing with ghosts. "I'm Harper Harlow. I'm from Whisper Cove. It's down the road a bit ... er, lake, a bit. Do you know where you are?"

"The Ludington Asylum."

"Right."

"I also know where Whisper Cove is." The woman floated a bit to her right, her eyes never leaving Harper's face. "You wear trousers."

It took Harper a moment to realize what the woman was saying. In her time, whenever that was, women mostly wore dresses and skirts. Pants were something men wore. And jeans? They were something no one wore in public unless it couldn't be helped. "Yeah. I like blue jeans. They're not as frowned upon in polite circles these days."

"Ah." The woman's smile was enigmatic. "I haven't been invited to any polite circles in quite some time."

"I bet." Harper wrinkled her nose as she considered sitting on a wooden chair, the creaking as she attempted to move it making her think better of the idea. "Who are you?"

"My name is Anna Pritchard." The ghost returned to hover in front of Harper. "I was a guest of this fine establishment for several years."

"It looks as if you never left."

"Nor will I ever."

"No, I guess not." The woman's quiet strength and calm unnerved Harper. "May I ask why you were sent here?"

"Seduction and disappointment."

Harper was sure she misheard the woman. "I'm sorry?"

"Seduction and disappointment," Anna repeated. "I got pregnant out of wedlock and my parents sent me here."

Harper barely managed to swallow her revulsion. In her head, she knew things like that happened. It seemed so out there given today's society, though, that she couldn't stop herself from being furious on Anna's behalf.

"You got pregnant so they sent you here?"

Anna nodded. "I worked at a restaurant after leaving high school. I was expected to find a husband, and fast, because my virtue was waning and I didn't have a lot of time."

"How old were you?"

"Seventeen."

Harper had trouble reconciling the number with the weary-looking woman in front of her. "How long were you here?"

"Five years."

Harper was positively apoplectic. "But ... how is that possible?"

"I had an affair with the diner owner," Anna explained. "He seemed nice and attentive. He said his marriage was over. He owned a business so I thought he was a good catch."

"Let me guess, you got pregnant and he didn't want to leave his wife. Am I close?"

"It turns out that his marriage wasn't in nearly the dire straits he pretended," Anna replied. "It also turns out that he didn't own the diner. His father-in-law did and let him run it and keep the profits. He only married his wife in the first place because his father-in-law promised him the diner in exchange for the proposal."

"Of course." Harper made a face. "So you turned up pregnant and told your parents?"

"I did," Anna confirmed, bobbing her head. "I thought they would force Gerard – that was his name, by the way, Gerard Hicks – into leaving his wife and marrying me. I wasn't aware of the situation until it was too late."

"What year was this?"

"It was 1949."

Harper did the math in her head, straining for memories from her high school history class. That sounded about right for the times. "So you got blamed even though he was an older predator and sent here? Why did they make you stay so long?"

Anna chuckled, the sound low and harsh. "Because I wasn't cured of my affliction."

"But ... ."

"I gave birth to a son about five months after I arrived," Anna explained. "It was ... in the basement." The way she said the words caused Harper's stomach to flip. She knew the basement would be awful, but she was starting to wonder exactly how awful.

"What happened to the baby?"

"He went to live with his father."

Now, in addition to being confused, Harper was angry. "So he got you pregnant, managed to get you locked up, and still claimed the baby?"

"That's my understanding, although they didn't tell me much," Anna answered. "Once I gave birth I was expected to forget what happened. I asked to see him, hold him. He was mine, after all. They never let me.

"I gave birth, heard him cry, and then they whisked him away," she continued. "He was given to his father and Gerard raised him with his wife. That's all I know."

Harper was understandably dubious about the story given the Ludington Asylum's checkered history, but she didn't voice her initial worry. That would make Anna's plight more unbearable. Deep down, Harper had a feeling the woman already wondered whether or not the baby ever the left the island.

"What about your parents?" Harper asked, turning the conversation to something more secure. "Why did they allow you to be sent here?"

"It was my father's idea. He was friends with Gerard and very upset when he heard I seduced the man."

"Seduced him? You were a teenager."

"Nevertheless, my father believed his friend," Anna supplied. "Initially I was only supposed to be sent here until I gave birth. My mother concocted a story about me visiting a sick aunt in Iowa. It was supposed to be a brief visit."

"They didn't come for you after the birth?"

"I never saw them again after the transport team arrived to take me," Anna replied. "I was going to run, you see. I was going to take the baby and raise him on my own. Of course, I had no idea how I was going to do it. I had a vague notion of freedom. It obviously never happened."

"So they sent a transport team?" Harper struggled to picture the scenario. "What, two men in white coats with a straightjacket?" It was her lame attempt at a joke – informed by watching hours upon hours of bad horror movies with Zander – but Anna's pitiful nod caused Harper's heart to seize up. "Seriously?"

"My mother let them in and then excused herself to have a drink in the salon," Anna said. "My father watched from the hallway as they wrestled me down, locked me up, and then dragged me out. They never came to see me even once after I left their house."

"But ... they must have sent letters." Harper had a difficult relationship with her parents – especially her mother – but she couldn't imagine either one of them simply abandoning her under any circumstances.

"Mail only came to the island once a month and none of it was ever for me."

The isolation must have been terrible, Harper thought. Anna was a young woman who did nothing wrong and yet she was terrorized for the choices of an older, predatory man. If Gerard Hicks was still alive she would've swam from the island to Whisper Cove to make him pay right about now.

"So you had the baby and they took him away." Harper swallowed hard. "Didn't you ask them why they weren't releasing you?"

"Of course, but Nurse Winstead was in charge of my wing and she didn't like questions," Anna explained. "In fact, if she thought you asked too many questions, she would ... punish you."

Harper wanted to ask how, but it seemed invasive. "So you stayed another four and a half years after that? I don't understand. Did you somehow slip through the cracks? How come you couldn't check yourself out?"

Anna snorted, genuinely amused. "My father had control of my fate until I had a husband to overrule him. I never had a husband so ... my father made the ultimate decision."

"And he chose to leave you here? You were his daughter. How could he?"

"He had three sons. He didn't need a daughter."

The response was so matter-of-fact that Harper had to bite the inside of her cheek to keep herself from letting loose with a torrent of obscenities that surely would've offended Anna. The story was horrible, sickening. It was also missing a very important piece of the puzzle.

"How old were you when you died?"

"Twenty-two. I believe it was three days after my birthday, but time became hard to mark within these walls."

Harper didn't doubt it for a second. "How did you die?" She was almost afraid to ask the question, but she had to know.

"I'm not sure." Anna pursed her lips. "I know I was supposed to be heading toward the hydrotherapy room, but I can't quite remember what happened when I got there."

That meant it was bad. "When did you wake up as a ghost?"

"A few days after. My things were already removed from my ward by then. There was a new occupant in my bed. I was confused, to say the least, but I was hardly alone."

Harper cocked her head, intrigued. "How many ghosts are here?"

"Numerous. How many ghosts can you see?"

Harper held her hands palms up and shrugged. "You're the only one in this room right now, at least as far as I can tell."

"You're not looking hard enough," Anna said, making a clucking sound to show sympathy. "There's more in this place than meets the eye. You shouldn't stay here."

"You shouldn't either," Harper noted. "I can help you pass over, if you want. I have a way to help you."

"Really? How?"

"It's a modified dreamcatcher that I built. It ... has power. It's hard to explain."

"And you can help me go where?"

"To the other side."

"What's there?"

"I honestly don't know," Harper replied. "I've only seen glimpses, but what I've seen is beautiful. It's better than this place."

"I will give it some thought." Anna shifted her head toward the back of the room, a tapping sound against the filthy window catching her attention. "Your friends will be here soon. Remember what I said about being careful, though. The souls left behind weren't all innocent."

It was a chilling warning and Harper understood what she meant by it. "Some of the residents really needed to be here, right?"

"And some were turned into people who needed to be here through no fault of their own," Anna said. "Whatever happens, don't come in here after dark. Bad things happen here when it's dark. Do you understand?"

Harper nodded. "Yes. I ... will I see you again? I want to help you if I can."

"I'm always around, but you're about to have other guests." Anna smiled as the glass shattered, her filmy countenance evaporating as fresh light flooded the room. "Remember what I said. Be safe. This place will take you, too, if you let it."

"Harper!" Jared almost tripped over his own feet in his haste to get inside of the room.

Harper stared after Anna for a long time before shaking herself out of her reverie and scurrying in Jared's direction. She threw her arms around his neck as soon as she reached him and Jared mistook the emotion for fear.

"Are you okay, Heart? I'm so sorry."

Harper smiled as she lifted her chin. "This place is full of ghosts. They're not all bad, though."

"Is that who you were talking to?" Shawn asked, curiously eyeing the empty room. "It didn't try to hurt you, did it?"

"No. She was nice. I'm going to try to help her."

"Great." Jared ran his hands over Harper's shoulders. "Don't scare me like that again, okay? I don't like it."

"I'll do my best."

## 8

## EIGHT

"We need to find the registration office."

Harper put up with Jared's coddling for exactly thirty seconds before she sprang to action. She had no idea if it was hearing the horrible things that happened to Anna or the fact that now she'd seen a ghost so she no longer had to worry about the initial introduction, but she was pumped.

"I need to hold you," Jared argued, refusing to let her go. "Come here." He buried his face in her hair, breathing in deeply. "I was afraid." The last part was barely a sigh.

Harper took pity on him and patted his back. "I'm okay. I told you I was okay when you were on the other side of the door. Speaking of that ... ." She flipped her gaze to the closed door, expecting it to magically pop open now that Anna was gone, but nothing happened. "Hmm."

"Hmm what?" Jared rubbed his cheek against Harper's soft skin. He didn't shave because they were camping so he had a bit of stubble going, something that Harper felt made him even more attractive.

"I thought Anna must have been the one to shut the door because she wanted to talk to me, but if that's the case, it should be open again, right?"

"I have no idea. Don't even think of moving away from me."

Harper was doing her best to refrain from shaking Jared, but she could only put up with so much. "Jared, if you get any closer people are going to think you're ... um ... mounting me in public."

"She's not wrong." Shawn did his best to look anywhere but their direction. "I would leave, but I'm not supposed to wander alone so I'm kind of stuck."

"Poor Shawn." Harper poked his side, amused. "I'm sorry you're forced to see this. He's just a little ... manic ... right now. He'll get over it."

"I won't." Jared hugged her tighter because he knew it irritated her and he was happy she seemed to have her fight back. "I think we should leave so I can do this at home."

"Oh, I think that's a very bad idea." Harper tilted her head back. "I'm angry now. I need to find the registration office."

"Why?"

"Because I need to look up Anna Pritchard's file."

"I would assume all of the files were transported off the island."

"And I would assume that's true, too." Harper tapped his wide jaw. "I would also assume that someone would take the couches and expensive antique chandeliers and yet they're still here."

Jared pursed his lips. "Will you tell me why this is so important to you?"

"Once we find the office, absolutely. I only want to tell the story once, though."

Jared blew out a sigh. "Okay. I think we can make that happen." He moved to walk toward the door and then remembered it was locked. "I wonder ... ." He scanned the floor, grabbing a piece of discarded metal and slipping it between the jamb and door. He barely tapped the metal in before the door sprang open, revealing a myriad of surprised faces on the other side.

"Thank you!" Zander hurried through the door, blowing past Shawn and not stopping until he stood in front of Harper. "Don't ever leave me again." He drew her into his arms, slapping Jared's hand away when he reached to rub her back. "I almost died without you."

"We were only separated for fifteen minutes," Harper pointed out.

"That's plenty of time to suffer a broken heart and die."

"Okay." Harper patted his back and pinned Jared with a gaze. "It's hell being loved sometimes."

Jared cracked a smile. "I bet. Now, come on. We'll find the registration office and you can tell us your story. After that, we'll regroup and discuss our next move."

"Wait ... what happened?" Michael asked, perking up. He'd been standing on the other side of the door with a dejected look on his face only moments before, clearly bored. He was back to being excited. "Did you see a ghost?"

"I did," Harper confirmed, ignoring the twin looks of doubt John and Steve exchanged as she breezed past them. "We need to find the registration office. I need to see if I can find patient files on Anna Pritchard."

"And who is that?" Steve asked.

"The ghost who warned me not to be in this building after dark," Harper replied. "She also claims the building is crawling with spirits and I believe her, because I'm pretty sure she's not the one who shut that door."

"The wind shut that door," John argued.

"Not from that angle it didn't," Jared said. "There's absolutely no way."

"Come on." Harper snapped her fingers. "I want to see those files and then I want some lunch. I think I'm getting my appetite back."

Jared followed her, grinning. "You still have to let me pet you later." He risked a glance at an intrigued Michael. "Not in a dirty way, you pervert. It's a love thing."

Michael didn't look convinced. "If that's your story."


**"THIS IS IT."**

Jared followed Harper back through the lobby, wrinkling his nose when she decisively veered to the left and pointed herself toward a small office. "How do you know that?"

"Because I looked at the plans."

"Oh." Jared grinned. "I thought you were going to tell me you had a feeling or something."

"I have many feelings. In this instance, though, I simply remember from the map."

Harper paid little heed to the debris on the ground, smoothly stepping over it and heading straight for a locked file cabinet. It was gun metal gray – or had been at one time – but now looked rusted throughout. Jared watched as Harper yanked on a drawer, enjoying the way she scowled when it didn't open.

"Do you want some help?"

Harper shook her head as she extended her hand. "Zander, do you have my thing?"

"Yup." Zander dug in his fancy man bag and pulled out a metal contraption Jared couldn't quite identify. "Here."

Jared narrowed his eyes. "What is that?"

"Tools of the trade."

"Get out of the way," Trey whispered, nudging Jared so he had no choice but to move out of the shot. "This is good stuff."

"Yes, I always love watching my girlfriend break the law," Jared muttered. "Why do you have a lock picking set?"

"If you knew what it was, why did you ask?" Harper held up the metal pins and selected one, leaning over and jamming it into the rusted lock before speaking again. "I need oil."

Jared was perplexed. "Oil?"

"Got it." Zander slapped a small bottle in Harper's hand. "I figured you would. I don't think that thing has been opened in forty years."

"Yes, but it's a big hunk of metal," Steve pointed out. "It's rusted. I guarantee there's nothing in there."

"Got it!" Harper's smile was smug as she graced Steve with a condescending look. "I bet there are files in here. What do you think, Zander?"

"I think you're always right, Harp."

"I do, too." Harper slid open the door, frowning when it put up a fight but ultimately breathing a sigh of relief when it opened with a groan of complaint. Inside, visible thanks to the window over the desk, were hundreds of files. "Huh. It looks like I was right."

Steve rolled his eyes, although Jared didn't miss the way his lips twitched. "How do you put up with her, man?"

Jared shrugged. "I think she's cute."

"Even though I break the law?" Harper challenged, digging into the file cabinet.

"We're going to talk about that lock picking set," Jared warned. "Prepare yourself."

"Somehow I think she's going to get away with it." Steve moved forward and grabbed a file, curiosity getting the better of him. "What do we have?"

"Patient files," Harper replied. "I had a feeling that not everything was removed when they closed this place down. Given the fact that all of the furniture was left behind, I think whatever happened was fast."

"Do you have any idea what that was?" Michael asked, selecting a file and flipping it open. "I can't remember reading anything about the asylum being shut down. I mean ... I know it was, but I don't remember reading specifics."

"People filed complaints," Zander answered, watching as Harper riffled through the files until she found the one she was looking for. "Is that Anna Pritchard?"

"Who is Anna Pritchard again?" John asked.

"The ghost who found me in the recreation room." Harper didn't care if the others thought she was crazy. She only cared about finding information. "She said she was locked up for seduction and disappointment – as if that's a real thing – and she gave birth here."

"She told you that?" Jared moved so he could read over Harper's shoulder, ignoring the way Trey vigorously gestured for him to stay out of the shot. "What happened to the baby?"

"It was a boy and she gave birth in 1949," Harper replied, her eyes busy as she roamed the data sheet. "She was told the baby was given to the father, but I'm understandably dubious given what we know about this place."

"Do you think they killed a baby?" Lucy was horrified.

"I have no idea," Harper replied, opting for honesty. "It's probably entirely possible that the father took custody of the baby. He was her boss at a diner. Gerard Hicks. He'd be long dead now but the baby ... ."

"Might still be alive," Jared finished. "I can find out. I can text Mel and ask him to look it up. I get zero service out here, but we can find out."

"I would appreciate that." Harper turned her full attention to the file. "This is her intake form."

"Wait ... you actually found a file on Anna Pritchard?" Steve was openly impressed as he looked over the lip of the file. "You did. Right there. It says she was locked up for seduction and disappointment. That is ... un-freaking-believable."

"It's also criminal," Harper said. "Anna told me that Gerard was friends with her father and her parents willingly had her committed for the bulk of her pregnancy because they needed to keep it a secret. Gerard told Anna his marriage was on the rocks and he was going to divorce his wife to be with her."

"Men never follow through on that promise," Lucy lamented.

"It was all a lie anyway," Harper said. "He didn't really own the diner. His father-in-law did and he would've lost everything if he tried to divorce his wife. So he knocked up a seventeen-year-old girl and fed her to the wolves."

"She was seventeen?" Jared was disgusted. "How could her parents have let that happen?"

"I have no idea, but Anna said that two men in white outfits showed up with a straightjacket and actually yanked her out of her house," Harper said. "She was going to run away. She said she had no idea how she was going to survive, but she was going to try and run. She never got the chance."

"So she ended up here," Michael mused. "What happened then?"

"She shouldn't have been here for more than a few months – her mother spread a story about her going to Iowa to take care of a sick aunt – and when she gave birth she was supposed to be released," Harper supplied. "She wasn't because she wasn't cured. She was here for five years, and she believes she died a few days past her twenty-second birthday."

"Wow." Lucy made an "o" with her mouth. "She told you all of that? Can it be confirmed in the file?"

"Most of it is here," Jared replied. "The birth is even listed and it says the baby was given to the father. There are some smudges at the end here, though. I think it says she died in December 1954."

"She doesn't know how she died." Harper rolled her neck. "She says she was supposed to go downstairs for hydrotherapy and she can't remember anything else. She woke up a ghost a bit later and someone else was already using her bed. She's been stuck here ever since."

"Does she want you to help her cross over?" Zander asked quietly, his eyes filled with sadness. "Did you tell her you can help make things better?"

"Cross over?" Finn cocked an eyebrow. "What does that mean?"

"Did you bring dreamcatchers with you?" Jared asked.

Harper nodded. "We brought a handful of them. Just in case, you know."

"I think you might be glad you did." Jared rubbed her shoulder. "It's going to be okay."

"I know." Harper smiled, her eyes lighting. "We'll be able to help Anna. She hasn't made up her mind whether or not she wants to cross over yet, but I think she ultimately will. She said the place is full of ghosts, though. She said I wasn't looking in the right place when I mentioned she was the only one I saw in the recreation room."

"What do you think that means?" Lucy hung on Harper's every word, mesmerized.

"I don't know yet," Harper replied. "I think I need some air, though. Let's take these files back to camp, grab some lunch, and discuss what we're going to do with the rest of the afternoon."

"I THINK WE SHOULD HIT THE BASEMENT NEXT." MICHAEL acted as if he'd been giving the matter serious thought before voicing his suggestion over crab salad sandwiches and potato chips. "It's the only logical step."

"And why is that?" Jared mimed patience, but Harper could feel the tension practically rolling off of him.

"Because that's where Anna died. She's the heroine of our story."

"I'm the hero of our story and I say that's a bunch of crap," Zander announced, wiping his mouth and shooting Trey a haughty look as the cameraman munched on a boring peanut butter sandwich. Zander was taking his feud with the man to new heights. "What do you think we should do, Harp?"

"Anna said she was due for hydrotherapy and that room was in the basement, but she didn't say she died there," Harper clarified. "She doesn't remember how she died. We need to give her time to remember."

"Will she remember?" Steve asked.

Harper shrugged. "It's different every time, but most ghosts remember eventually. If Anna has truly been blocking it out for this many years, it might be worse than she can bring herself to remember. We can't push her."

"That was a very dramatic trick you pulled off in there," Finn noted, taking great pleasure in munching on his crab salad in full view of Trey. "How did you know about Anna Pritchard? Did you read about her in one of the news articles?"

Harper shifted so she could study the man. "She told me."

"Yeah, and that makes great television. How did you really know?"

"She told me," Harper repeated.

"Harper is the real deal," Jared said, balling up his napkin and slipping it into a garbage bag. "I'm sure you've dealt with a lot of frauds over the years, but Harper is not one of them."

"But ... ." John risked a glance at Michael, snapping his mouth shut when the producer shook his head in warning.

"Don't make me take that sandwich away from you," Zander ordered, his temper flaring.

John held up his hand palm out. "It was a simple question."

"And she's answered it," Jared said.

"Yeah, yeah." John shook his head. "I have no intention of pushing you on the situation. It's just ... the whole thing is so fantastical."

"And it's going to keep getting more fantastical," Harper announced, wiping her hands off on the seat of her jeans as she stood and faced the asylum. "I'm not ready for the basement. I think we should check out the kitchen and dining areas next. We can go over some of the files by the campfire tonight, see if there's anything good in them, and then make a plan for tomorrow after that."

"That plan had better include the basement," Michael grumbled.

"We'll see." Harper refused to give him the answer he wanted. "Let's see what else we can find, huh?"

"How come you're so much more gung-ho now than you were this morning?" Trey asked, tossing his plate before reaching for his camera. "You acted as if you were afraid of this place a few hours ago and now you're eager to explore."

"I wasn't sure what to expect this morning."

"And now you know what to expect?"

Harper shook her head. "There's something bad in that asylum. I have no doubt about that. The fact that someone good like Anna could survive without being swallowed whole, though, gives me hope that it's not going to be as horrible as I initially envisioned."

"I hope not," Lucy said, missing the dark look crossing over Jared's face. "That won't make very good television."

"Don't worry." Harper gripped Jared's hand to keep him from spouting off. "I have a feeling you're going to get some really great television before the end of the weekend."

"And what are you going to get?" Finn prodded.

"I don't want anything but to help a few displaced souls find closure," Harper answered. "If I get that, I'll be perfectly happy."

She meant every word, even if the members of Michael's group didn't believe her in the slightest.

## ❦ 9 ❦

## NINE

L unch was an excitable affair, Lucy and Michael energetically discussing what Harper discovered and how they could use it to their advantage. Trey and Finn spent the bulk of their rest time checking their equipment and grabbing special lights to enhance filming abilities inside the asylum. Molly and Eric loosened up enough to smile at everyone else in the group – although they continued glaring at one another – and Zander's crab salad was a big hit so everyone was happy with the food.

Only Jared seemed taciturn.

"What's your deal?" Harper joined him by the water while everyone else cleaned up and gathered their belongings.

Jared tipped his head and shrugged. "What makes you think I have a deal?"

"You're thinking too hard not to have a deal."

"Maybe you're my deal." Jared flashed a smile as he playfully grabbed her around the waist and tugged her into his arms, but Harper knew him well enough to know that it was a forced effort.

"Tell me."

"Heart ... ."

"I thought we weren't going to keep secrets from each other,"

Harper prodded, going straight for his jugular. "Isn't that what we promised one another?"

Jared's handsome face twisted into an angular scowl. "You know how to kick me where it hurts, don't you?"

"I would never do that. Hurting you there hurts me over the long haul."

"Ha, ha." Jared flicked the end of her nose before resting his forehead on hers. "I'm ... confused."

"About me?"

"In a manner of speaking."

Harper expected a different answer so she jolted. "What did I do?"

"Heart, you didn't do anything," Jared chided, gathering his patience and control. "It's just ... you were terrified of this place two hours ago and now you're gung-ho to go back inside and look around. I think you're even softening about going into the basement."

"I didn't say I would definitely go into the basement," Harper hedged.

"No, but I saw the look on your face," Jared countered. "It was thoughtful, as if maybe you could get persuaded. You get the same look on your face when you say you're not hungry, but Zander says he has ice cream."

Harper pinched Jared's arm. "That is a horrible thing to say about the woman you love."

"I don't believe teasing you about your eating habits reflects the depth of my love."

"Then tell me what's bothering you and I'll see if I can fix it," Harper suggested. "That would be an example of me showing you my love."

"You're on a mission."

Harper widened her sea-blue eyes. "Excuse me?"

"You're on a mission," Jared repeated, refusing to back down. "You've decided to help Anna no matter what. Now that you've met someone who isn't all bad in that place – and I think you had yourself convinced all of the spirits inside would be somehow evil or twisted – you want to see how many of them you can help."

"That's not a bad thing because I absolutely love your huge heart," he continued. "It worries me, though, because you tend to act before you think when your heart gets involved."

"Is that what I did when I fell for you? Act before I thought?"

"Yes." Jared bobbed his head. "I did, too. I never considered myself a rash person until I met you and I knew almost right from that first moment that I had to have you."

Harper was absurdly warmed and embarrassed by the sentiment. "You thought I was a quack when you first met me."

"I *wanted* you to be a quack when I first met you," Jared corrected. "You weren't and here we are. I knew that you were something special even though if I'd really thought it through the sensible side of me would have insisted on taking things slow."

"Do you wish we would've gone slower?"

"No. Not for one second. Do you?"

Harper shook her head. "I knew when I saw you, too. It was as if I was struck by lightning or something."

"That doesn't change the fact that I need you to be careful," Jared said. "I fell in love with you because of your big heart. It will kill me if that big heart somehow results in you getting hurt or … worse."

Harper didn't need to ask what "worse" he referred to. "I'll be careful. I promise." She leaned forward and pressed a soft kiss to the corner of his mouth. "Now, come on. I want to see the kitchen. I'm hoping Anna pops up again. I'm hoping she can introduce me to other ghosts right away."

"See, that's not being careful." Jared shook his head as he watched her scramble away. "That's the opposite of being careful."


**"LOOK AT THE** EQUIPMENT IN HERE."

Molly was tickled as she ran her hands over the antique stove. The front door was rusted through, the remnants hanging by a lone hinge, and the grates on top of the stove were missing.

"Can you believe people used to cook on something like this?" She was enthusiastic when she looked to Harper.

Harper shrugged. Industrial ovens didn't whip her into quite the frenzy they apparently did Molly. "I don't cook so I don't have a lot of interest in the stove."

"She doesn't need to," Zander explained. "I cook for her."

"Yeah, explain that to me," Steve prodded, walking around the dark kitchen and pitching his flashlight beam to various spots as he searched the floor. "Harper and Jared date. They don't just date, in fact, they're clearly infatuated with each other. You have a boyfriend who you're tight enough with to go on a haunted vacation together. Yet you and Harper live together. How come?"

Zander shrugged, unbothered. "Because we've been best friends since kindergarten."

"That doesn't really answer the question," Steve pointed out.

"Because we wanted a house and neither of us had money to buy one without help," Harper supplied. "At the time, we were both single so buying a house together didn't seem to be such a big deal."

"And now?"

"And now ... we're a happy foursome," Harper replied, unsure how to answer. Steve seemed interested in drumming up trouble and she didn't want to give him ammunition. "I don't see what the problem is."

Steve didn't immediately respond, instead flicking his eyes to Jared. "Doesn't it bother you? Wouldn't you like to share a roof with your girlfriend?"

"I've only been in Whisper Cove for six months," Jared replied, his tone even. "The living arrangements are fine for now."

"But what happens when you want to marry the blonde?"

"Then I'll start ring shopping."

Harper made a strangled sound in the back of her throat and the look Jared spared her was full of annoyance rather than understanding.

"Don't worry. I haven't started ring shopping. You have time," Jared said, rolling his eyes.

"That's right," Zander supplied. "Jared knows better than to go ring shopping without me."

"I do?"

Zander nodded without hesitation. "I'm the one who knows what type of ring she's been dreaming about since she was in middle school."

Jared stilled. "Good point. I *do* know better than to go ring shopping without Zander," he said. "As for now, the living situation is fine. We spend every night together, whether at their place or mine. Zander and Shawn split up their time between two locations, too. No one is in a hurry to change things."

"Well, at least you have a plan," Steve drawled.

Unbelievably uncomfortable, Harper grappled for something to talk about that didn't revolve around a ring and possibly moving. "So, who else thinks the really old stove is awesome, huh?"

Molly wrinkled her nose, disgusted. "You just said you didn't care about it."

"People can change their minds," Harper shot back. "That's what happened here. I changed my mind. I happen to find that stove ... fascinating."

"It must be a woman thing," Trey noted, shaking his head as he filmed the stove. "I don't see anyone else buzzing about the stove. It has to be hormones or something."

"Definitely," Steve agreed. "How about you, Lucy? Do you like the stove? You're the only other woman here so you have to answer."

Lucy didn't do as instructed, causing Harper to flick her eyes to the spot where she could have sworn the woman stood when they entered the room. The area was bare, though, and a quick scan of the kitchen told her Lucy was nowhere to be found.

"Where did she go?" Jared asked, catching on to Harper's unexpressed worry.

"She was just there a few minutes ago," Zander offered. "I know because she saw a spider and we both crossed ourselves to make sure it didn't fly at us."

Eric snorted. "Spiders don't fly."

"I guess you haven't seen *Arachnophobia*." Zander folded his arms over his chest, obstinate. "Spiders most definitely fly."

"We'll talk about your love of bad movies later," Harper said dismissively, nudging Zander to get him to move so she could get a better look at the room. "Jared said everyone is supposed to have a buddy and yet Michael is here and Lucy isn't."

"Where is your buddy, Michael?" Jared queried, his shoulders squaring as he shifted from tour taker to detective. "She was supposed to be with you at all times."

Michael, who had been listening to the conversation with mild disdain, held his hands out. "She was here a second ago. I wasn't really paying attention to her."

"Don't you think that's your job?" Jared challenged.

"I think I'm her boss," Michael replied, his tone clipped. "It's my job to make sure that we have a good show when this is all finished – which is not going to happen if we don't go in the basement – and that's what we were talking about not more than fifteen minutes ago. She probably went down there to scope it out."

Jared's spine stiffened, his temper threatening to erupt. "So you sent her down there to make us look for her?"

"I most certainly did not." Michael tugged on his pastel Polo shirt to smooth it. "She didn't mention going down there. I just assumed she did."

"We're getting ahead of ourselves," Steve said, stepping between Michael and Jared in case they came to blows. "She might've simply slipped out to use the restroom."

"That's a good point." Jared gripped Harper's hand. "We should probably go back out to the main foyer to see if we can find her."

"She wouldn't go to the bathroom there," John argued. "None of the facilities in this place would work now and even if they did, well, would you sit on a toilet in here?"

Harper involuntarily shuddered when she considered it.

"Speaking of flying spiders," Eric muttered.

"Then we'll check outside." Jared moved his jaw as he decided what to do. "In fact, we'll split up. Our group will search outside and you guys can search inside."

Michael balked. "How is that fair?"

"She's your team member," Jared answered, refusing to back down. "Our team members stuck together as they were supposed to. Your team members do whatever they want while spouting rude crap every five minutes."

"What does the rude crap have to do with anything?" Zander asked, genuinely curious.

"It just bugs me."

"Fair enough." Zander crossed his arms over his chest. "I agree with Jared. We'll check outside and you guys handle inside. If we find her, we'll make sure you know it."

"But ... ." Michael didn't look as if he favored the idea at all. "You want us to go into the basement without the ghost whisperer? She's here to talk to the ghosts."

"Yeah, maybe the ghosts can help her," Trey deadpanned, rolling his eyes.

"Not only are you not getting chicken tonight, but the cookies I plan to bake under the stars will be out of your grasp, too," Zander hissed.

Trey's mouth dropped open. "You're making cookies?"

"Remind me to always go camping with you," Jared said, tugging Harper so she wouldn't make a mistake and volunteer to stay behind and search the asylum with Michael's team. If she tried, they would have a big fight. He wasn't looking forward to it, but he wouldn't shy away from it either.

"Now I kind of want to go camping with him and I always thought camping was for idiots," Eric noted, falling into step behind Jared.

"You think everyone who isn't you is an idiot," Molly muttered, drawing Harper's curious eyes as the woman scuffed her feet against the floor. "You're so smart and everyone else is dumb. We get it."

"Do you have something on your mind?" Harper asked, catching Molly by surprise.

"Um ... no." Molly pressed her lips together and dragged a restless hand through her short-cropped hair. "Let's go outside and look for Lucy."

"Yell out if you find her," Jared ordered, leading the way out of the kitchen. "We'll do the same."

"But ... ." Michael was flustered. "Don't you think you should search the basement? We'll send a camera crew with you if that makes you feel better."

"We're good," Jared said. "Be careful when you search. This place is haunted, after all."

**JARED WAITED UNTIL** HIS SIX-MEMBER TEAM WAS FULLY accounted for outside to begin speaking.

"I don't like this one bit."

"I never would've guessed," Harper said dryly, her lips twitching as her eyes darted around the open expanse of the island. "I don't see Lucy here."

"I don't understand why she left without telling anyone," Eric argued. "If she had to go to the bathroom, why didn't she tell that windbag Michael?"

"Maybe she didn't want to go in front of him," Shawn suggested. "Zander won't go to the bathroom in front of me because it makes him uncomfortable. They have different parts. Maybe she was embarrassed."

That was an interesting idea, although Harper wasn't convinced. "Then why not ask Molly or me to go with her?" she challenged. "By the way, that bathroom thing is a sign of respect. I don't go to the bathroom in front of Jared either."

Shawn looked to Jared for confirmation.

"She doesn't," Jared agreed. "It's not that I'm weird and want to watch her or anything, but she won't even talk through the door when she's in there. She pretends she can't hear me."

"The bathroom is a private place," Harper hissed.

"I hear that." Zander offered Harper a fist bump. "Why don't people get that?"

"I guess we must be slow or something," Jared drawled. "As for the rest, I want everyone to break up and search the island for signs of Lucy. Do not go back in that asylum. Harper and I will take the boat."

"We will?" Harper didn't bother hiding her surprise. "Why?"

"Because I want to check something," Jared replied. "Don't split up. Stay with your partner."

"Oh, joy," Molly muttered.

"I'm not kidding." Jared extended a warning finger. "I don't like this. At all. It feels wrong. That said, I don't think they're above generating their own sort of publicity so I want to check on something before they get the chance to embark on a cover-up."

"You don't think she's dead, do you?" Shawn was horrified at the prospect.

"Probably not," Jared replied. "She's probably hiding and this was simply an effort to get Harper into that basement. By the way, until she shows back up, the basement is out of bounds. I'm not rewarding them for bad behavior."

Harper sensed his distress so she wisely kept her mouth shut even though she wanted to point out that if Lucy was somehow taken by one of the ghosts, she might very well end up in the basement through no fault of her own. Jared wasn't ready to hear that, though.

"We'll meet back at the campsite in thirty minutes," Jared said. "Stick together."

Harper had to struggle to keep up with Jared's long strides as he turned in the direction of the boat. She huffed and puffed a bit as she broke into a run, growling when he refused to slow down even though she knew he heard her toiling behind him. "You're really worried, aren't you?"

"I'm ... concerned." Jared hurried down the dock, helping Harper on the boat before following her over the side.

Harper had no idea what he was looking for so she merely stood back and watched as he strode into the small cabin and picked up the radio.

Jared was calm as he turned the dial, trying every frequency on the board before slamming his hand down in frustration.

"What's wrong?" Harper knew nothing about boat communication, but Jared clearly wasn't happy.

"The radio isn't working."

"Maybe the boat needs to be on for that."

Jared's glare was withering. "Heart, I love you more than anything, but that's not how a boat works."

"How was I supposed to know that?"

Jared adjusted his tone. "The radio should work regardless. I don't know a heck of a lot about boats either, but this one has no juice for the radio."

"Will the engine still start?"

Jared pursed his lips. "That's a good question." He strode to the central spot where the ignition was located and found the key missing. "I wonder who has it."

"Maybe they were simply worried someone would steal the boat," Harper suggested.

"Or maybe your buddy Michael wanted to make sure that we were unable to leave the island while he played his little game," Jared said, extending his hand. "Come on. There's one other thing I want to do while we're alone."

"Now is *so* not the time for that."

Jared wasn't happy, but he managed to muster a genuine smile. "We can always find time for that. Just ... not right now. Come on. We don't have a lot of time."

## ✷ 10 ✷

## TEN

"Where's the boat key?"

Jared wasn't messing around when the groups met up in the asylum's foyer forty minutes later.

Michael, much paler than when they left, slapped Jared's hand away when the police officer patted the side of his shorts. "Do you mind? I believe that's a private area."

"Only if you're hung like Michael Fassbender, which I sincerely doubt," Zander quipped, shrinking back when Michael murdered him with a diabolical look. "Or ... maybe you are."

"Where's the boat key?" Jared repeated, his temper getting the better of him.

"Why do you want the boat key?" Steve asked, his face impassive. "If you want to leave, I can't allow that until we find Lucy."

"We're not all leaving," Jared clarified. "Only one of us is leaving."

"Who?"

"Eric." Jared jerked his thumb in the stoic equipment manager's direction. "He's going back to Whisper Cove to get us some backup. Apparently the radio isn't working correctly so we need to get our own help."

"I am?" Eric's eyebrows hopped up.

"You are," Jared confirmed. "I tried texting Mel from the beach. I got minimal service out there last night, but I have no bars now. Since the radio isn't working, that doesn't leave us with a lot of options. I want help on this island."

"Why don't all of us head back?" Eric argued. "Wouldn't that make more sense?"

"We can't leave Lucy," Molly scoffed, ignoring Eric's pronounced eye roll. "She could be in trouble."

"Or this could all be part of a bit," Jared corrected.

"What is that supposed to mean?" John leaned against one of the foyer's filthy walls, arms crossed over his chest. It was a clear sign he was going to put up a fight, but Jared was beyond caring. "As for the radio, it was acting funky during the trip out here. I thought it would hold, but I guess it didn't."

"It means that I haven't ruled out the prospect that Michael and Lucy set this up to get Harper into the basement," Jared replied, not missing a beat. "They had their heads bent together at lunch and they could've easily plotted this. I'm assuming you didn't find Lucy when you looked."

"No, we didn't." John softened his stance a bit. "I can't just let you take the boat. It was rented with production company money. Only an employee is allowed to drive it per the contract."

Harper risked a glance at Jared, cringing when she saw the nerve working in his jaw. "What if John goes back with Eric?" she suggested. "That way Eric won't be alone and the company will be represented."

"I didn't agree to that," Michael argued.

"No one asked you," Harper snapped, taking the producer by surprise with her vehemence. "Did you and Lucy work this out so you could get me into the basement? I want to know."

"Of course not."

Harper wasn't convinced. Michael had one toe in the Hollywood waters. Sure, it was a small pool that was more Hollywood-adjacent than anything else, but she was convinced he knew how to lie. "Did you look in the basement?"

"Well ... ." Michael wrinkled his nose.

"He refused to go down there without you," Steve supplied. "He said the professional ghost hunter should be in charge of that particular hunt. We did go up to the second floor."

"And?"

"And as far as I can tell, she didn't head that way," Steve replied. "There's a layer of dust – and what looks to be mold because part of the ceiling has caved in and it's rained up there – but it doesn't look to me as if anyone has walked in that area. We called around and did a quick search, but we didn't have any luck."

"And why didn't you go to the basement yourself?" Jared challenged.

"Because Michael told me not to and he's still technically my boss."

The answer didn't make Jared happy in the least. "Oh, well, that's brave." Jared blew out a frustrated sigh as he ran a hand over the back of his head. "Okay, John, you should go with Eric."

"Why don't I take Steve with me?" John suggested.

"Because I might need Steve here," Jared replied. "As far as I can tell, Steve and I are the only ones with any training. I think Shawn will be some help, too, but I want as many strong bodies as possible and with you and Eric leaving, that means I only have three."

"Hey!" Zander was offended.

"I mean four." Jared held up his hands in a placating manner. "I wasn't suggesting you're not buff and strong."

"Just brave, right?"

Jared pretended he didn't hear the question. "I need at least one member of the security detail here. In fact, if one of the camera crew members would prefer going to Whisper Cove, that would be even better." Jared slid his expectant gaze to Trey and Finn, but Michael answered before they could.

"Absolutely not," Michael snapped. "I need them to film the search for Lucy. This could be the most exciting thing that's ever happened on our show."

"And that right there is why Jared is suspicious of you," Harper noted, shaking her head. "Lucy is missing. You don't seem worried in the least."

"Of course I'm worried," Michael countered. "It's just ... I'm sure she's fine. She probably simply got turned around."

"Why don't I think that's how you're going to play it for television?" Jared muttered, absently rubbing his hand up and down Harper's back. "If one of your people has to go, it will be John and he'll go with Eric."

Michael opened his mouth to respond, something snarky clearly on his lips. Instead he regrouped and offered up a curt nod. "Fine. John and Eric can go back to Whisper Cove and get backup. Then, when the backup arrives, we can all feel foolish together because we'll have already found Lucy."

"That would be great." Jared shifted so he faced Eric. "Go straight to Mel. Tell him what's going on. He'll know what to do."

Eric nodded, somber. "Are you sure you don't want me to stay? You could send Molly back with John."

Jared spared a glance over his shoulder before drawing Eric away from the group so they could talk without anyone overhearing. "I'm not comfortable sending her off with a guy I don't know." Jared's voice was barely a whisper. "John seems like a nice enough guy. He's not one of the snarky ones but ... ." He left it hanging.

"But she would be trapped on a boat with a guy who could be a pervert or something," Eric finished, his eyes briefly locking with Molly's before he forced his attention back to Jared. "It's going to storm tonight. You felt it outside. What if I can't get back here tonight?"

"Then get back here first thing in the morning," Jared replied. "I can hold it together for one night. At least I hope I can."

"Do you really believe something happened to Lucy?"

"I honestly don't know," Jared replied. "I wouldn't put it past Michael and Lucy to set something like this up, but Harper feels that there are numerous ghosts in this place. Just because the first one she met was nice and pleasant, that doesn't mean the remainder of them are."

"Right. Okay." Eric rolled his neck until it cracked. "I'll be back as soon as I can. I won't let you down."

"I know you won't. Even though you don't like me, you love Harper and Zander. I think you're even fond of Molly, although you don't want to admit that and you're acting really odd where she's concerned. Just for the record ... I know what's going on."

Eric's kept his face blank. "Oh, yeah? What's that?"

"Something you don't want to admit to, but you will eventually," Jared replied, not missing a beat. "Go before it gets too late. I'll take care of things on this end."

Eric opened his mouth to add something, but Jared stopped him.

"Yes, that includes taking care of Molly," Jared said. "Go. I don't like any of this right now and I want more people I trust on this island."

**"THIS WAY."**

Harper knew Jared wasn't keen on going to the basement – he wanted to force Michael's hand and make the overzealous producer admit that this was all a setup – but she realized that venturing into a more dangerous part of the building was practically a necessity at this point.

"We'd better not be going to the basement," Jared grumbled, doing his best to ignore Finn as the cameraman trailed them. They agreed to leave everyone else together in the foyer, for protection, and handle the next leg themselves. Jared still wasn't sure how he felt about it.

"We're not going to the basement," Harper said. "There's one more room on this floor we haven't looked at. It's on the other side of the common room."

Jared knit his eyebrows. "What room? I don't remember seeing it on the plans."

"That's because it was essentially an open space on the indoor plans," Harper explained.

"You're saying it wasn't on the plans."

"Basically."

"So how do you know it's there?"

"Because, when we walked outside, I noticed the wall was built out in one spot and it didn't make a lot of sense to me," Harper replied. "That's the spot that's empty on the plans. I remembered it after we took a second loop around the island looking for Lucy."

"So you think whatever Bennett built there is something that he didn't want anyone to see," Finn mused. "That's cool."

"I was going to say something else but ... whatever." Jared reached forward and looped his finger through one of Harper's back belt loops. "Don't even think of walking through whatever door we find without me."

Harper snorted, enjoying the levity given the heavy situation. "I'll do my best."

"You will do more than that," Jared said. "I'm going through the door first. Me."

"What if the door slams shut and we're separated again, just with you on the other side this time?" Finn asked.

"I ... yeah, we're going in together." Jared eyed the large door he missed on their first pass through the main floor. "Huh. I guess I must've assumed this was a janitor's closet."

"Oh, it is." Harper's eyes sparked with excitement. "I think the back of the closet it what leads to the other room."

"I'm still not sure I'm buying there's a secret room here," Jared offered. "I looked at the same plans you did and didn't notice a thing."

"That's because you weren't looking for the same thing I was."

"Which is?"

"Secrets," Harper replied, reaching for the door handle. "This whole place was built on secrets and lies. The hospital administrators managed to ruin entire lives because they kept secrets."

"Heart, what happened to Anna was tragic, but it was also fairly normal for the time in question," Jared pointed out, bracing himself when the door swung open. If she moved to step forward he was prepared to drape himself over her as a shield if it became necessary. "Women were treated as property back then."

"Ah, the good old days," Finn teased, grinning when Harper glared at him. "What? Bad joke?"

"Don't push her too far," Jared warned, keeping a firm hold on Harper as she stepped into the tiny room. "See. It's a closet."

"It is," Harper agreed, swinging her flashlight to the back wall and grinning when she saw a second door. "It's a closet with two exits. How often do you see that?"

Jared's stomach twisted when he realized she was right. "How could you possibly have guessed that?"

"I told you. I looked at the building plans."

"I guess that will be good if you two ever want to buy a house together," Finn teased.

"Shut up," Jared grumbled, keeping close as Harper walked through the second door.

The room they found themselves in was much bigger, and unlike the foyer with its missing windows and ravaged wooden floors, this room was largely untouched. Jared kept one hand on Harper to make sure he didn't lose her in the dark and flicked on his flashlight. Harper followed suit and Finn increased the illumination on his camera. Then all three of them gasped in tandem.

"Holy ... what is this?" Jared asked, dumbfounded.

"It's a treatment room," Harper said around the lump in her throat. "Some of the patients were ... um ... treated in here."

"I think you mean tortured," Finn corrected, zooming the camera toward the tiled floor. "What is that?"

"What?" Jared jerked his head in the direction Finn filmed.

"It looks like blood," Finn murmured.

Jared squeezed Harper's hip before taking a step in that direction, kneeling next to the discoloration and pressing himself closer to the ground so he could study it. Unlike the rest of the asylum, this room was pristine. It reminded Harper of a museum exhibit rather than an abandoned torture chamber.

"I'm pretty sure it is blood," Jared said after a beat.

"Lucy?" Finn sounded frightened.

"No, it's not fresh." Jared ran his finger over the tile. "It's very, very old."

"So what is this room?" Finn asked, swinging the camera toward the back wall. "Look. There are tools hanging over there."

Harper saw them before Finn and was already moving in that direction. She stopped next to a wooden bench – one that looked as if it belonged in a garage rather than a medical room – and studied the assortment of metal devices hanging from hooks on the back of the bench.

"What is that?" Jared almost jolted Harper out of her skin when he appeared at her back. "Sorry, Heart." He sensed her momentary distress and kissed the back of her neck. "I didn't mean to frighten you. I thought you heard me come up behind you."

"It's okay." Harper forced a bit of bravado into her voice. "I know what this is." Harper pulled down an odd-looking device. It had a blunt head on one end and a wicked point on the other. She grabbed something that looked like a small hammer and held the two items together. "I know what this room was used for."

"I'm almost afraid to ask," Jared muttered, shaking his head. "What are those?"

"They're used for lobotomies," Finn answered, making a clucking sound in the back of his throat. "I did a lot of research on asylums before this trip. I'm guessing this was some sort of behavior modification room."

"What kind of modification?" Jared asked, horrified.

"It could've been anything," Harper replied, struggling to find her emotional footing. "Seduction and disappointment was only one ridiculous thing people were accused of back in the day. There were others."

"Like?"

"Like masturbation, menstrual derangement, religious enthusiasm, desertion of husband, and even jealousy. There were tons of them."

"Huh." Jared wasn't sure what to make of the list. It sounded made up, but he was positive it wasn't. In a way, he found it funny. Of course, he was standing in a place where it was treated as anything but funny and people suffered because of it. Jared wisely opted not to laugh, but he couldn't stop himself from making a lame joke. "I guess it's good your menstrual derangement period is still a few weeks off, isn't it?"

Harper rolled her eyes but managed a slight giggle, which was all Jared really wanted. "I guess it's good for you that you're over that whole Jason thing, too, right?" Jason Thurman was a former boyfriend who recently returned to Whisper Cove and opened a restaurant. Jared still found himself getting jealous when Jason looked at Harper in a certain way, even though he fancied himself ridiculously secure in their relationship.

"Menstrual derangement is worse."

"It is not."

"It is so."

"It is not."

"It is so."

"It kind of is," Finn hedged, chuckling when Harper swiveled to face off with him. The laughter died on his lips when he saw her face go ashen. "What the ... ?"

Harper fell backward – away from Jared – and hit the tiled floor with an audible "oomph."

"Heart?" Jared was only mildly concerned, figuring she must've gotten her feet tangled together or something. He immediately changed his mind when Harper's eyes rolled back in her head and she began twitching. "Harper!"

Jared dropped to his knees, unsure what to do. "Is she having a seizure?"

"How am I supposed to know?" Finn asked, his voice squeaky. "I'm not a doctor."

"I don't know what to do." Jared was near tears. "Heart, please open your eyes." He gingerly ran his fingers over the back of her head looking for an injury of some sort.

Instead of answering, Harper rolled her head from side to side, small gasps escaping. Jared was relieved to see movement, but the feeling only lasted a few moments because then she started to scream.

And she didn't stop when her body began thrashing about. The terrifying sounds only got worse. Much, much worse.

## ELEVEN

"**H**arper!"

Jared was anguished as he held tight, terror overwhelming him as he debated what to do. As far as he knew, Michael didn't have anyone with medical training in his group. Thankfully for him, Harper wasn't out of it for long. When she returned to the land of the living, though – and Jared was convinced something truly horrible happened to her while she was out of it – she was confused.

"Jared?"

"Harper." Jared let loose with a strangled gasp. "It's okay." He stroked her hair as he rearranged himself on the floor, tugging her onto his lap as he pressed her tight against his chest. He ignored the fact that he was sitting two feet away from what he believed to be dried blood and instead focused all of his energy on his blonde. "You're okay." He pressed a kiss to her forehead.

"What should I do?" Finn's face was white as he knelt. "Should I get help?"

"No," Harper answered immediately. "I'm fine. Besides, we can't split up. Jared said so."

Jared wasn't keen on having his words thrown back in his face –

especially given the fact that Harper's body was just now ceasing to shake – but he didn't argue with her. "Stay with us. Although, if you film her, I will break that camera."

Finn glanced at the expensive piece of equipment he held in his hand and shrugged. "I don't own it." He held up a hand when Jared opened his mouth to say something snide. "I'm not going to film her. I'm just as freaked out as you are by what just happened."

Jared doubted very much that was the case, but he had no intention of wasting time arguing. "Heart, what happened to you?"

"I'm not sure." Harper ran her hand over her cheek as she searched her memory. "It's weird. What did you see?"

"I didn't see much," Jared replied. "One second you were fine and the next you were on the floor."

"That's not completely true," Finn hedged. "I happened to be looking at her when it happened and she went rigid. Her eyes went wide before they rolled back in her head. I swear it looked as if she saw something."

"Did you see something?" Jared focused on Harper.

"I don't know." Harper struggled to find the right words to express herself. "Something was there. I think ... I think it was a man, but I didn't get a chance to focus on him before I started seeing ... um ... other things."

"What other things?" Finn was genuinely curious. "Did you see other patients?"

"It wasn't like that," Harper hedged. "It was different. Usually I see spirits in this world. They know they've been left behind – or they at least expect it – and their reactions are appropriate to the time. That's not what I just saw."

"Heart, if you don't tell me what you saw I'm going to have an aneurysm or something," Jared admitted. "I thought Zander was the king of the meltdowns. I was wrong. I'm about to take the crown."

Harper forced a smile as she reached up and ran her index finger down his cheek. He caught her hand and pressed the palm to his strong jaw.

"Tell me, Heart."

"I saw ... something ... from the past," Harper said after a beat. "I saw a memory, I think. It was something that happened in this room."

Jared involuntarily shuddered as he flicked his eyes to the work-bench with the lobotomy tools. "Did you see what those were being used for?"

Harper pressed her eyes shut and searched the memory. "I don't think so. That wasn't the focus."

"What was the focus?" Finn asked.

"It was a man," Harper replied. "It was a doctor. I think it was Bennett, but I can't be sure. I want to ask Michael if he has a photograph of him because it's been years since I've seen one and I'm not sure I would recognize him."

"Bennett?" Jared wrinkled his nose. "I thought you said that he disappeared once the state shut down the hospital. He left the area without being arrested ... or paying for what he did."

"That's the story, but he wasn't technically a ghost," Harper said. "At least, well, I don't think he was a ghost. I saw something else. It wasn't ghosts."

"What was it?"

"A memory."

Jared wasn't sure what to make of the simple declaration. "You saw someone else's memory?"

"I think the building has a memory." Harper answered the question, but she was talking more to herself than Jared. She couldn't understand what happened and yet her theory seemed to be the only thing that made sense. "I think a lot of evil was done inside of these walls and it marked the space."

Jared had no idea what that meant. "What did you see, Heart?"

"Like I said, it was a doctor. I'm pretty sure it was Bennett. He was arguing with a nurse about treatment courses for ... sexual derangement."

Jared tightened his arms around Harper's small frame. "Is that a reference to what we did Saturday night?"

It took Harper a moment to realize he was trying to make her laugh, and even though the joke was lame, she indulged him because she needed it as much as he did. "You were just a garden variety pervert on Saturday night. I believe sexual derangement was more for ... homosexuality."

"Oh." Jared stilled as his mind wandered to Zander. "Did you see someone die in this memory?"

"No." Harper shook her head. "The nurse was arguing with the doctor about his treatment plan. She said she thought it was too harsh, but the doctor didn't agree. That's all I saw ... other than them preparing the tools. Trust me. That was more than enough."

"Okay." Jared pressed a kiss to Harper's cheek and pushed her to a standing position before joining her. He kept one arm around her waist as he glanced around the dark room, flicking his flashlight in every corner to make sure they didn't miss anything. "Lucy isn't in here."

"And given the way the room looks – how preserved it is – I don't think she's been here," Finn added. For the first time since joining their little excursion, he looked somber. "Do you think she's dead?"

"Of course not," Jared answered automatically.

"I don't know," Harper said, shaking her head. "I guess it depends on where she is and who she's come into contact with."

Finn cocked an eyebrow. "Meaning?"

"Meaning that she might very well have left of her own volition at the beginning," Harper replied. "She's been gone a long time, though. Would you hang around this place waiting for a television crew to find you? I think fear would've gotten the better of her at a certain point, don't you?"

Jared shifted his eyes to Harper's face. "So where do you think she is?"

"I honestly have no idea," Harper replied, leaning into Jared as he led her toward the door. "I'm going to guess the Ludington Asylum had a lot of secret rooms."

Jared was in no position to argue with her, so he didn't.

By the time they reached the foyer, he was ready to admonish Harper and Finn not to play up the story too much because he didn't want to create a panic with the other group members. Instead of finding everyone huddled together and talking, though, he found Molly and Michael staring through the open front door.

"What's going on?" Jared released Harper and hurried forward. "Has something else happened?"

As if on cue, a deafening roar of thunder caused the room to rumble. Harper instinctively pressed her chest against Jared's back in an effort to chase away the sudden burst of fear coursing through her.

"Storm," Michael replied, barely sparing a glance for them. "It's going to be a doozy. The others went to save as much of the camping equipment and food as possible."

"And you decided to help, huh?" Jared asked dryly. He was really starting to dislike Michael. He wasn't a fan from the first meeting, but the man fell in his estimation with every breath.

"Someone had to watch Molly," Michael protested.

A bolt of lightning flashed across the sky and another rumble of thunder followed. Thankfully the rain hadn't yet started, which meant they still had time to save as much of the camping equipment as possible.

"Stay here, Heart," Jared ordered, striding toward the door. "I will be back as soon as possible."

Harper anticipated his reaction and was on his heels before he hit the front walk. "I'm going with you."

"Stay here," Jared repeated, annoyance flashing.

"Don't bother arguing," Harper shot back. "I'm going with you and that's the end of it."

Jared opened his mouth to argue and then snapped it shut. In truth, he preferred keeping her close even if they both did get wet. He didn't trust the asylum, especially after Harper's "episode" in the treatment room. "Okay, but you stick close to me."

"That's the plan."

"That's the way it's going to be forever," Jared corrected, increasing his pace. "Now, come on. The storm is almost here."

**HARPER AND JARED** WERE THE LAST TO MAKE IT INSIDE, grabbing several sleeping bags and the pile of pilfered files from the registration office before racing into the asylum under a deluge of rain. They were soaked when they hit the foyer. Zander, however, had grabbed their bags and they both had changes of clothes inside that were not wet.

Shawn set about hanging the sleeping bags over benches and chairs so they would dry while Jared and Harper began peeling off sticky items of clothing.

"Turn around," Jared ordered when Finn, Steve, and Michael turned their interested faces in Harper's direction as she tackled her wet jeans.

"I hardly think we're looking in a nefarious manner," Michael scoffed.

"Turn around or I'll pop you in the face," Jared growled, his patience fraying. "I'm already not happy about you sitting inside while everyone else did the work to gather the provisions."

"Someone had to stay with Molly," Michael argued.

"You made me stay with you because you didn't want to go outside ... or be left alone," Molly argued.

Jared briefly rested a hand on Molly's shoulder to calm her. He'd already figured that out himself. "It's okay. Can you help Harper change her clothes, though? I will make sure that no one is looking from this side."

Molly flashed a thumbs-up. "Got it."

Jared fixed his attention on Michael, practically daring the man to so much as glance in Harper's direction as she stripped. Jared considered taking her into another room, but ultimately decided against it because he didn't want to isolate her. "If you even think of looking at her ... ."

"I hardly think I'm some sort of demented pervert," Michael scoffed. "I happen to be quite popular with women on my own. I don't need to go after another man's girlfriend. I don't need to go after anyone, for that matter. People always come after me."

Jared wasn't convinced. "If you look at her, I'm going to make you cry in front of your workers. I'm just warning you now."

"Cry?" Michael was confused. "How are you going to do that?"

"I believe he's going to use his fists," Finn said, heaving out a sigh as he set down his camera and lowered himself into one of the uncomfortable wooden chairs near the wall. The chair was rickety and ugly, but it was a much better option than anything with fabric. "Do you think we're stuck inside all night?"

"I think that's probably the case," Jared confirmed, trying to tune out Molly's murmurs as she aided Harper. "Even if the storm blows over, the ground is going to be wet and the tents are bound to be blown all over the place. Some of them might end up in the water and the others will be tattered."

"So you want to sleep inside?" Shawn pushed Zander so their backs were to Harper and Molly, but they were spread out enough – shoulder to shoulder with Jared – that they cut off almost all view of Harper as she changed. "Do you think that's safe?"

"I don't see where we have a lot of choice in the matter," Jared admitted, tugging his damp shirt over his head and hanging it on a nearby table. "Eric and John are in Whisper Cove. That storm outside is producing huge swells. That means that they're not going to be able to come out here until the morning. There's no way Mel will risk a boat in these waters. Once it's dark ... they'll come at first light if they can. Not before."

"I still think you're overreacting," Michael argued. "Lucy is probably perfectly fine."

"Oh, yeah?" Jared offered up a dark glare. "Then why hasn't she found us? Why hasn't she given up this ridiculous game and rejoined the party?"

"Because she's probably in trouble," Harper answered, freshly dressed as she moved to Jared's side. "I think she most likely went off on her own as a way to entice me to the basement. She would've been back by now, though, if she was still okay. Something else is happening."

"So we clearly need to head to the basement," Michael pressed. "We have to find Lucy right now."

"That's one possibility," Jared conceded, ignoring the fact that Molly openly gaped at him as he unbuttoned his jeans and shimmied out of them. He didn't care who saw him naked. Zander and Shawn had already seen the show – and didn't care in the least – and Molly was young and enthusiastic and bound to buck up his ego. He had no problem with that. "The other possibility is that we wait through the night and hope Mel brings a lot of reinforcements with him when he comes."

"I don't think that's a good idea," Michael argued. "What if Lucy is hurt? What if she fell down?"

Harper cast Jared a sidelong look. "He's right. We can't not look."

Jared blew out a sigh. He was afraid she would say something like that. "Heart ... ."

"No." Harper shook her head, firm. "Lucy probably did wander away to manipulate me. That doesn't mean she's not in over her head now. We have to at least try to look for her, find her. If it was me, I wouldn't want to be the one abandoned in this place."

"If it was you, we wouldn't be in this position," Jared muttered, dragging a restless hand through his hair. Even though he wanted to argue, he knew it was a lost cause. Harper couldn't leave Lucy without knowing and, truthfully, neither could he. "Okay. We're going to have dinner and then we're going to go through the basement as a unit. It's going to be one quick pass ... no investigating."

"Of course we have to investigate," Michael sputtered. "That's part of the show."

"Then you can stay down there and investigate," Harper shot back. "We're going to look for Lucy. We're not going because we care about your stupid show."

"I still care," Zander said. "I think I would make a marvelous television star. Lucy is more important, though."

"Lucy is definitely more important," Harper agreed. "We're going to look for her because it's right. I will not be performing on cue, though."

"That's right." Zander puffed out his chest. "She's not a trained monkey."

"I am starving, though," Harper said. "Zander, I don't suppose you can make your fancy fried chicken in here, can you?"

"Oh, Harp, I can do anything I set mind to."

Harper beamed. "That's exactly what I'm counting on."

## TWELVE

The storm made the asylum feel even gloomier than normal. Once their wet clothes and the sleeping bags were left to dry, Harper and Jared moved to chairs so they could watch Zander work his magic with dinner. Molly, who was a bundle of nerves, volunteered to help and Zander happily allowed her to take on a few tasks ... under his strict supervision, of course.

"You don't have to go to the basement," Jared said, keeping his voice low as he collected Harper's hand and pressed it to his chest. "You can stay up here with Zander and Molly and I'll take Shawn and Steve with me to check the basement. In fact, I think that would be a safer course of action."

"No."

Harper's answer was so succinct Jared did a double take. "No?"

"No," Harper repeated. "I don't want to be away from you right now and I need to see for myself. You know that."

Jared heaved out a sigh. He *did* know that. "I had to try."

"I know, but you would've changed your mind."

"Oh, really? How do you know that?"

"Because you're too afraid of being separated from me in this place," Harper replied, her pragmatic side taking over. "On one hand you want to protect me. That means, at least in your mind, keeping me out of the basement. On the other you know you need to be close to protect me so you wouldn't have actually left me without adult supervision."

Jared pursed his lips to hold back a smile. "Molly is an adult. I would've left you under her supervision."

Harper returned the smile. Now, an hour past her ordeal in the treatment room, she was feeling more like her normal self. "Molly is acting weird."

"She has green hair. What was your first clue?"

"Not that." Harper playfully slapped Jared's knee. "I think something happened with her and Eric."

Jared shifted his shoulders, intrigued and yet wary. "Like what? Do you think they secretly did it or something? I would be totally for that, by the way."

"Only because you think Eric is still interested in me."

"He *is* still interested in you."

"Not in the way you think," Harper corrected. "He might have a minor crush on me, but he's moved on. I think that before we started dating he honestly believed he had a shot."

"Did he?"

"No."

"Did you think I had a shot when you first met me?"

Harper grinned, Jared's question serving as a form of amusement despite the dour circumstances. "I think the moment I met you I thought you were kind of a jerk so that would be a no."

"How long did you think I was a jerk?"

"A good twenty-four hours after the first time I imagined you naked."

Jared snorted, amused. "That sounds about right."

"After that, though, I think I knew. I think Eric knew, too, which is why he hated you so much at the beginning. You guys seem to get along better now, though."

"I wouldn't say we're friends," Jared clarified. "He's not a bad guy, though, and I trust him to get the job done. Why do you think he's the one I sent back to Whisper Cove?"

"I think there were a variety of reasons for that, but the main one was that you wanted a member of our team in charge and you were afraid to let Molly go by herself," Harper replied. "You also wanted Zander and Shawn here because you think they're good backup should something happen to you."

"Oh, you're so smart." Jared poked her side. "I do want you to have loyal people around you at all times, though. I'm not going to lie about that."

"And I'm going to be really angry if something happens to you," Harper countered. "Make sure that doesn't happen."

"Right back at you." Jared leaned forward and pressed a kiss to her lips. "I want to hit the basement as soon as we're done with dinner. The faster we do it, the faster we can set up shop here. It's not exactly safe but ... it's our only option."

"Yeah." Harper rolled her neck. "Have you considered the worst possible scenario?"

"What is that?"

"That she's dead and we'll find her body in the basement."

"I *have* considered that," Jared confirmed. "If that happens ... well ... at least we'll know. That's not the worst possible scenario. The worst possible scenario is that we never find out what happened to her. That will haunt both of us."

Harper leaned so her head rested against Jared's shoulder, smiling when he brushed his lips against her forehead. "That's another reason I know you would've changed your mind when it comes to separating and searching the basement. Not knowing what happened to me if I disappeared would be worse than knowing I died."

"No, it wouldn't," Jared said. "Knowing you died would ... I don't ever want to consider that. It would be worse."

"I don't know," Harper argued. "I don't know what happened to Quinn and it froze me in place for a very long time even though I knew he and I weren't going to make it over the long haul." She referred to a boyfriend who died in a car accident years before, his body never found. Jared knew the story. He also knew that she remained haunted by the fact that she was convinced Quinn's soul was out there and she wanted to make sure she put him to rest.

"I didn't consider that, Heart," Jared conceded. "I know you struggled with that. I know you still feel guilt over it even though there's nothing you can do to change it. If you died, though, I would be inconsolable."

"I feel the same way about you." Harper squeezed his hand. "I love you."

"I love you, too." Jared flicked his eyes to the fireplace Zander was using to cook his gourmet meal. "Do you think he can pull this off?"

"I think Zander can pull off anything he sets his mind to. I hope this chicken is as good as he promised. I really am starving."

"Eat up. You're going to need energy to tackle the basement."

Harper had no doubt he was right.


**"WHY ARE YOU** BRINGING CAMERAS?"

Jared was in a relatively good mood thanks to Zander's chicken as they gathered at the top of the stairs that led to the basement. The feeling was fleeting when he saw Finn and Trey readying their equipment.

"Because this is a television show," Michael replied. "We're supposed to be filming so that's what we're going to do. This is going to be a very compelling episode."

"Yeah, it's going to be great," Jared muttered.

"Ignore them," Harper said, tying her hair back in a ponytail as she readied herself for the descent. "It doesn't matter. It's not our concern. We have to find Lucy. That's where our focus should be."

"Shouldn't their focus be on Lucy, too?" Jared challenged. "She's their co-worker."

"If you think we're not worried about Lucy, you've severely misjudged us," Michael argued. "Why do you think I pressed so hard to go to the basement?"

"Because you know that's where the truly terrible stuff happened and you want to see Harper perform like a trained monkey," Jared replied. "She's not going to do that, for the record. We're going downstairs to look for Lucy. That's all."

"She signed a contract," Michael persisted. "She has to talk to ghosts."

"Yeah? I looked at that contract. It's null and void if either party faces an emergency," Jared said. "I think a missing crew member constitutes an emergency."

"But ... ."

"Shut up." Jared didn't bother masking his disdain. "I'm sick of this conversation. I happen to know a few lawyers who will rip that contract to shreds. Don't push me on this."

"Dude, you should totally have a T-shirt made up with that saying on it," Finn teased. "You say it a lot."

"Well, I happen to mean it." Jared switched on his flashlight. He changed out the batteries before dinner because he wanted to make sure it didn't accidentally die. Once the beam flared to life, he grabbed Harper's hand with his free one. "Stick close to your partners. Molly, you stick close to Shawn and Zander. They're your new partners for this little trip."

Molly nodded, her eyes filled with fear. She was usually gung-ho when it came to ghost excursions, but she looked beaten down by recent events.

"What about me?" Michael asked. "I don't have a partner either."

"I don't care if the ghosts take you," Jared replied. "In fact, maybe they'll be up for a trade. We'll get Lucy back and leave you down here for the night."

"That sounds like a splendid idea," Shawn enthused.

"I get absolutely no respect from you people and I don't like it at all," Michael grumbled.

Jared ignored him as he descended the stairs, his senses on high alert. He considered finding a piece of rope and tying Harper to him for the trek through the dark and dreary space, but ultimately figured she would put up a fight if he tried. Instead he warned Shawn and Zander to keep a close watch on her and hoped things would turn out for the best.

That's all he felt he could do.

Harper's eyes were keen as she swished her flashlight through the darkness. The basement smelled of mildew, wet dirt, and blood. She hoped she was imagining the last one, but she had her doubts.

"I already hate it down here," she murmured.

"You're not the only one." Jared's hand was sweaty, but he refused to let go of Harper's hand. "Don't you wander away from me."

"I won't."

"Promise me."

"I promise, Jared." Harper meant it. "I'm afraid to be too far away from you right now. I think this place has the potential to swallow me whole."

Jared felt sick to his stomach at the admission. "I wish we'd never agreed to do this."

"Me, too. I think the problem is that I would've always second-guessed myself if we hadn't."

"Well, it's done now." Jared flicked his light to a door and narrowed his eyes as he tried to read the lettering on the window. "All we can do is try to make it through so we have a terrifying story to tell our children one day."

Harper stilled. "Children?"

"Are you about to tell me that you don't like kids?" Jared tucked his flashlight under his chin so he could open the door without releasing Harper's hand. He grabbed the flashlight and slowly scanned the room before turning his full attention to Harper. Her pretty face was devoid of makeup and hauntingly pale due to the limited light. He still thought she was the prettiest woman he'd ever met in real life, but her ashen features worried him. "If so, we're going to have to discuss that later."

"I don't dislike kids," Harper noted. "I'm just surprised you're talking about them here."

"Here was not the best place to talk about them," Jared admitted. "I'm just glad we're on the same page."

"I didn't say that," Harper cautioned. "How many do you want?"

"One or two." Jared was blasé when he answered. "If the first one is loud and mouthy – which is a distinct possibility given our attitudes and his delightful Uncle Zander – I might be happy to stop there. Otherwise, I've always pictured myself with two kids."

"A boy and a girl?"

Jared shrugged. "I can't control that. I just want healthy kids. If we have two girls or two boys, I can live with that."

Harper couldn't help being impressed. "Most men would rather hide under a truck than admit what you just said."

"I'm not most men."

"I know. That's why I love you."

"Oh, geez." Trey made a disgusted sound in the back of his throat. "Why don't you guys just strip and start making these imaginary kids right now?"

"You're back on the naughty list," Zander hissed. "I gave in and let you have chicken because I felt sorry for you, but no more. You can eat dirt for all I care."

"It's okay, Zander." Harper moved to the next door and opened it, mimicking Jared's earlier actions as she searched for signs of Lucy. The room was empty other than a metal table in the center of the room. It looked like an operating table, which made Harper's blood run cold and her mouth turn dry. "Nothing."

"Everyone check each room," Jared ordered, his eyes locking with Shawn's as the gym owner crossed in front of him. "I want to keep this orderly but move fast. I don't want to be down here when darkness falls outside."

"How come?" Michael asked, speaking for the first time since they hit the basement. "I would think that's the best time to be down here to catch paranormal activity."

"I'm sure it is." Jared's voice was flat. "We're not going to find out, though."

"I think we should leave that decision to Harper," Michael challenged, refusing to back down.

Harper responded without hesitation. "We're not staying in this basement after dark. Anna warned me not to be in the building after dark. It's bad enough we have to sleep here, but I won't be in the basement during the overnight hours."

"But ... ."

Harper was firm. "Period."

"That goes for our entire group," Zander added. "If Harper believes

Anna, she has a reason to do it. I believe Harper because she's almost always right."

"When am I not right?" Harper asked, suspicious.

"Whenever you go lingerie shopping," Zander replied. "I've told you a hundred times to let me pick out your naughty stuff, but you never let me. You're always wrong when you don't let me, by the way."

Harper turned her attention to Jared, irritated. "Tell him there's nothing wrong with my lingerie."

"There's nothing wrong with her lingerie," Jared automatically answered, his attention on the way his flashlight bobbed around the room he searched. "It's fine."

Harper balked. "Fine? It's supposed to be better than fine."

"I prefer you naked. Lingerie is too much work."

Harper rolled her eyes. "Sometimes I think you're extremely lazy for a dedicated cop."

"You're not wrong." Jared knit his eyebrows. "Heart, what is that thing?"

Harper moved closer and focused on the item that caught Jared's attention. "It's a hydrotherapy closet. Er, well, I think that's what they're called. I honestly can't remember."

"How does it work?"

"The two doors open up and the patient gets inside so only their head sticks out through the opening at the top. Then the bad vibes and nasty thoughts are steamed out of them."

"So they're kind of boiled?" Jared was horrified.

"Not exactly," Harper clarified. "Hydrotherapy is one of the few practices from back then that's still utilized today. It's beneficial for sweating out toxins and stuff. It does not, however, cure mental disease. Zander and I like to take a steam at the gym when we go."

"Hmm." Jared risked a glance over his shoulder and met Shawn's gaze. "Watch Harper a second."

"What do you mean?" Harper was confused when Jared released her hand and stepped closer to the hydrotherapy closet. "Where are you going?"

"Not far," Jared replied, purposely keeping his voice level so Harper wouldn't panic. "I need to look inside."

Harper realized what Jared wasn't trying to say and broke away from Zander when he tried to put an arm around her shoulders. "You think someone could've hidden a body in there, don't you?"

Jared scowled when he realized Harper followed him inside. "I just want to be sure. Go back to Zander."

"No." Harper moved her hands to the locking mechanisms on top of the device. "Have your flashlight ready and don't panic if I scream."

"Scream?" Jared arched an eyebrow. "Why would you scream?"

"Because I'm imagining rats running out of here."

"Oh, well, in that case, don't panic if I scream either."

Harper flashed him a thankful smile, sucked in a breath and then shoved open the sides of the device. She held her breath as she waited for little squeaks to overtake the room. There was nothing, though, including a body.

Harper giggled as she let loose with a shaky exclamation. "Whew."

"Whew is right," Jared said, recapturing her hand as he exhaled heavily. "Okay, let's keep looking. I want to get this search over with as soon as possible. The longer we stay, the more we risk something bad happening. Let's finish this."

## 13

## THIRTEEN

"**H**ere."

Zander handed Harper a s'more – even though she didn't ask for it – and settled next to her on the floor. The group did their best to clean off a space where they could camp, but the foyer remained filthy and there was very little they could do about it.

"Thanks." Harper accepted the snack but didn't immediately set about to eating it. Her stomach remained upset from the two hours they spent searching the basement ... and coming up with absolutely nothing. "I'm not sure I'm hungry."

"Eat it," Jared ordered, taking the spot next to her. "You love s'mores."

"I do but ... ."

"Harper, you can't beat yourself up about this," Jared chided. "Lucy wasn't in the basement. I'm not sure she was ever in the basement. You're not going to find her because you decide to forego your treat."

Harper exhaled heavily. She knew he was right, but she couldn't stop the worry and dread from overtaking her. "Where do you think she is?"

"I don't know." Jared opted for honesty. He wasn't keen on lying but would do it if he thought it would make her feel better. In this particular case, though, he knew she would see through any attempt. "This place is so big that she could be right under our noses."

"Maybe we should look at the plans again," Harper suggested. "We might see places where hidden rooms should be."

"I will agree to that if you eat your s'more."

Harper glanced at the gooey goodness in her hand and made a popping sound with her lips when her stomach growled.

"See, you really want it," Jared prodded. "I know you feel bad and don't want to enjoy anything while Lucy is missing, but you can't stop living. I promise that we won't leave until we know what happened to Lucy."

Harper took a bite of the s'more, not bothering to wipe the chocolate from the corners of her mouth as she munched. "You can't promise that."

"I can," Jared argued. "It's a small island. If we have to tear down the asylum to make sure we find her, we'll do it."

"What if she's not on the island, though?" Harper held the s'more so Jared could take a bite, which he did.

He methodically chewed as he considered the question, swallowing before answering. "What do you mean by that? Do you think she somehow left the island?"

Harper shrugged. "It's a possibility, isn't it?"

"I guess but ... how? She wasn't on the boat. It's not big enough for anyone to hide."

"Maybe she swam," Zander suggested. "She could've decided that this place was too creepy and thought that swimming back to the mainland was a good idea."

"That's miles away."

"The nearest island isn't that far," Zander argued. "You can see it from the west shore."

"Yes, but it's fall," Jared pointed out, offering Shawn a manly chin bob as the man sat to Zander's left and began eating his own s'more. "The water is too cold. She would've died from hypothermia before she got there."

"It's not that cold," Shawn argued. "I saw a report on the local news a few days ago and it said, because the fall has been so warm, that the water temperatures in Lake St. Clair are higher than normal. It takes an extended cold snap to lower water temperatures. It hasn't been great the past two days, but that's hardly an extended cold snap."

Jared rolled his neck, his mind busy. "Give me another bite of that, Heart."

Harper did as he instructed, popping the last bite into her mouth as she watched him internally puzzle things out.

"Okay, let's say she could survive the swim," Jared said after a beat. "She looked to be in decent shape so she could probably swim the distance as long as the water didn't get too choppy. Why would she want to do something like that?"

"Maybe because she and Michael came up with a plan," Shawn said. "He was desperate to get Harper in the basement and you were against it. He knew you would win in the end and he needed to force the situation. They might've thought it was easy manipulation and that was the best thing they could come up with to make sure you guys didn't discover her and ruin the episode."

Jared ran his thumb over Harper's lip, wiping at the chocolate remnants. Then, even though he was preoccupied, he leaned forward and kissed the corner of her mouth, removing the remains of the chocolate.

Harper giggled as he held her still. "You could've handed me a napkin."

"This is a lot more fun." Jared did the same with the other side of her mouth before releasing her. "I don't doubt that Michael and Lucy could've come up with a plan to make it so Harper had no choice but to go into the basement. They seemed desperate to get her down there."

"Yeah, and did you see Michael's face when he realized Harper didn't see any ghosts?" Shawn asked. "He was bitterly disappointed. He watched her the entire time."

"How do you know that?" Zander asked.

"Because I noticed it right away and I decided to watch him for hints," Shawn replied. "He had Trey at his side and a finger ready to point in Harper's direction. He never got to pull that trigger, though."

"That's because the basement was empty," Harper noted. "I didn't see or even sense anything else down there. It was dark and depressing, don't get me wrong, but there weren't any ghosts."

"And yet you said before that you sensed a lot of ghosts." Jared tucked a stray strand of Harper's hair behind her ear. "When we first got here, in fact, you were a little withdrawn because you sensed so many souls milling about. Where did they go?"

"They're still here," Harper replied. "They simply weren't in the basement when we were there. I mean, technically I guess they could've been there watching us, but if they were they didn't want to be seen."

"Why?" Jared absently ran his fingers over her back, the need to keep in constant contact with her somewhat distracting. "I would think these souls have been trapped here, alone, for so long they would enjoy playing with new guests. Isn't that why you and Zander have jobs in the first place? Ghosts like to draw attention to themselves."

"They like to throw rotten apples, too," Zander muttered, shaking his head.

"Especially at people who move when they're not supposed to move," Harper said.

"Don't go there." Jared wagged a warning finger. "Now is not the time to fight."

"When is the time to fight?" Zander asked pointedly.

"You guys can fight to your heart's content when we get off this island," Jared answered. "In fact, if you want to fight to the point where you can't share the same roof, I'm sure Shawn and I could come up with a way to separate you for a few days."

"Oh, we can't be away from each other for days," Zander countered. "One night will probably suffice, though."

"Days is too long," Harper agreed. "One night might work."

"I guess I'll take what I can get," Jared said. "Go back to the ghosts, though. Why wouldn't they want to be seen?"

"I don't know," Harper replied. "That's a good question, though. I have no idea why they would want to remain in the shadows like this. I don't get the feeling they see a lot of visitors, although your theory about kids partying on the island might prove me wrong."

"Still, that would just be a summer thing," Jared noted. "It's definitely too cold for them to be out here in the winter and if they get to enjoy a month or two in the spring and fall that would be the maximum."

"Maybe they're afraid," Shawn interjected, swallowing hard when three heads swung in his direction. "I just mean that ... they were probably afraid in life because they were being mistreated. Maybe they're afraid in death, too."

"That's not a bad theory," Harper mused, reaching to rub her sore neck. Jared brushed her hand away and dug his fingers into the tender flesh there. "Maybe something is controlling them."

"What could that possibly be?" Jared asked, legitimately curious.

"I don't know. I want to look at those plans again, though."

"I'll grab them."

"You can finish your massage first," Harper said, grinning when Jared lobbed a rueful smile in her direction. "Please."

"You're lucky I love you," Jared muttered. "Still, I think looking at the plans and picking out specific places to search tomorrow is our best option."

"I think surviving the night and getting backup is our best option," Zander corrected. "I'm not convinced this is going to be an easy-breezy evening."

"Why is that?"

"Because Anna Pritchard warned Harper not to be in here after dark." Zander jerked a thumb to the window, where the sun was barely visible as it made its inevitable descent into the horizon. "I don't happen to think that was an empty threat."

Jared remained calm, but an involuntary shudder ran down his spine. "I forgot about that."

"Yeah, well, let's just say that I think it's going to be an eventful night," Zander said. "I also think we should forego any hanky panky and sleep close to one another."

Jared made an exaggerated face. "I can guarantee I would never do hanky or panky under these conditions."

"I totally would if I wasn't so afraid," Zander countered. "Fear shrinks my manhood, though, so I'm totally out tonight."

Jared blinked several times in rapid succession before focusing on Harper. "We're definitely going to have separate couple's nights when we get back to Whisper Cove. I'm warning you now."

Harper giggled, delighted. "I can live with that."


**HARPER WOKE** TO BRIGHT SUNSHINE FILTERING THROUGH THE window above the foyer and Jared wrapped tightly around her. They shared a sleeping bag since they didn't save enough for everyone to have their own when the storm hit, but it worked out fine because Harper felt safe the entire night.

Other than her dreams, of course. Her dreams were bloody and disturbed. Thankfully she only thrashed about once before Jared managed to lull her back to sleep.

"Nothing happened," she murmured, realization washing over her. She'd been so tense the night before because she assumed the ghosts would run wild during the overnight hours that she had trouble falling asleep. She was so exhausted, though, she couldn't fight off slumber. Now, in the bright light of day, she felt a bit silly.

"What?" Jared stirred next to her, lifting his sleepy head. "Is something wrong?"

"No. Nothing is wrong." Harper struggled to a sitting position and glanced around the room. They were the only ones awake as far as she could tell. "Nothing happened."

Jared rubbed the sleep from his eyes and regarded her with a lazy smile. "That's good, right?"

"It's ... odd," Harper replied, lifting her arms over her head so she could stretch. "I expected something bad to happen. I'm not going to lie."

"I'm just glad it didn't." Jared trailed his fingers down Harper's arm. "Come here and cuddle with me for a few minutes. Once everyone gets up we won't have a chance for any alone time."

"That hasn't stopped you before," Trey called out, smirking when Jared jerked his chin in that direction. "You two are a walking billboard for sexual chemistry."

"I'll take that as a compliment," Jared said dryly. He sat up, resigned that his morning plans weren't going to come to fruition. There would be no soft kisses and roaming hands in his immediate future. "No one heard anything?"

"I slept hard," Trey said, his hair standing on end as he sat and looked around. "I had weird dreams, though."

"You did?" Harper was intrigued. "What did you dream about?"

"You and your boyfriend putting on a sex show for everyone and the gay dude withholding food while everyone watched."

Harper scowled. "You're a sick man."

"It's not my fault you guys won't stop petting each other," Trey shot back. "You're the ones who made my mind go wonky."

"Whose mind went wonky?" Finn asked, joining the conversation. Compared to everyone else he looked relatively put together, although that wasn't saying much because he had bags under his eyes. "Are you guys talking about weird dreams? I had one, too."

"What did you dream about?" Harper was almost afraid to ask, but she couldn't stop herself. "If it's sexual in nature, you can keep it to yourself."

"It wasn't sexual." Finn wrinkled his nose. "It was weird. I kept hearing kids talking."

"Kids?" Jared rolled his neck before moving his hands to Harper's back to give her a morning massage. She always enjoyed a vigorous morning rub, and since they slept on the hard floor he naturally assumed this would be no exception. "Why would you dream about kids?"

Finn shrugged. "I have no idea. I heard them talking – even crying – and then I heard adults telling them to be quiet."

"Were kids ever housed here?" Jared asked Harper.

"Yeah. They had a children's ward. I don't believe they ever had many of them at one time, though. Visiting was difficult and most children weren't considered violent offenders."

"They had a children's ward?" Michael furrowed his brow as he sat.

He looked to be a slow riser, which was fine with Jared because the last thing the agitated policeman wanted was another fight, especially before Zander served breakfast. "I don't remember reading about that."

"It didn't get a lot of press," Harper explained. "Plus, I don't believe any children ever went missing. The local story – the one from the St. Clair newspaper – said that only five or six children were ever housed here and they were all accounted for when the state came in and started removing patients."

"That doesn't mean they weren't mistreated," Jared pointed out. "If Bennett was as sick as you say, it sounds as if he was doing experiments on people."

"It does sound like that, but he might not have seen it that way," Harper countered. "In his mind he was probably conducting medicine. The things we find so abhorrent about this place were considered common back then. You have to remember, they didn't know the things we do now."

"I still don't know how anyone thought a lobotomy was acceptable medical practice," Jared grumbled.

"I don't either, but I believe they're still done in some instances today," Harper said. "I don't know exactly what they are, mind you, but I swear I read about it in a newspaper article from not that long ago."

"Well, there went my appetite." Jared grabbed a small piece of discarded wood from the floor and chucked it in Zander's direction, smirking when he heard the annoyed man groan. Zander and Shawn shared a sleeping bag, too, although they were both muscular men so they didn't have as much room to move around as Harper and Jared. "Get up."

"Go away," Zander complained, tugging the sleeping bag over his head. "I need my beauty rest. We've been over this."

"We have." Jared was clearly enjoying himself. "We've talked about it almost as much as we've talked about the fact that I don't like it when you crawl into bed with us on weekday mornings."

"He crawls in bed with you?" Trey smirked. "How ... cozy."

"No one asked you," Zander spat, rolling to his back. "Harper and I like to gossip in the morning. It's our ritual. We do it in bed because we live in Michigan and it's warmer that way."

"I guess I can see doing it when it was just the two of you, but now there's four of you," Trey pointed out. "Doesn't that get crowded?"

"Oh, I don't crawl into their bed with them," Shawn offered, showing his first signs of morning movement. "I find the entire thing weird. I'm still getting used to Harper climbing in bed with us when Jared has to get up for an early shift."

Jared stilled, surprised. "Really?"

"Oh, geez." Harper averted her gaze. "Do we have to talk about this?"

"You said it was always Zander who did that," Jared pressed. "Come to find out, you both do it. I feel so ... betrayed. You lied to me." He wasn't really angry so he poked her side in a playful manner. "You're going to have to make up for the lying later. I'm going to think of a punishment for you, and I don't want to hear any complaints when I do."

"Whatever." Harper yawned as she focused on the empty sleeping bag on the other side of the spot where Zander and Shawn slept. "Who's missing?"

"What do you mean?" Jared was only half listening, his mind traveling to punishment possibilities.

"Molly." Harper's body stiffened. "Where is Molly?"

Jared read the worry in her voice and tore himself out of his perverted reverie. "What do you mean?" He rolled to his knees and glared at the empty sleeping bag, taking a moment to count heads before swearing under his breath. "Did anyone see Molly get up in the middle of the night?"

"No." Trey poked Steve in the side to wake him. "Hey. We're missing another one."

"We don't know that yet," Zander protested, his face flushing with color. "She could've just run out to go to the bathroom. It's sunny out." He said the words, but he wasn't convinced.

Jared crawled to Molly's sleeping bag and ran his hand over the interior. It was cool to the touch. "She hasn't been here in quite some time." He risked a glance at Harper and saw her eyes flooding with tears. "Son of a ... . Okay, everyone get up. We have another man down."

"Woman," Shawn corrected. "We have another woman down. We officially have one woman left in our group."

Jared's stomach twisted. He hadn't put that together. "Okay, we're starting a search and we're starting it right now."

## ❦ 14 ❧
## FOURTEEN

"**C**ome on."

Jared grabbed Harper's hand and dragged her behind him as he headed for the door. He tried to maintain a calm demeanor despite his worry, mostly because he was convinced Harper would never get over it if something terrible happened to Molly and he didn't want her to see the fear coursing through him.

"Search the outside of this island very carefully," Jared ordered, his eyes briefly locking with Shawn's, something unsaid passing between them. "Do not go back inside the asylum unless we're together. Do you understand?"

Shawn mutely nodded and clapped Zander on the shoulder to propel him to move to the west side of the island. Instead of doing that, Zander shuffled closer to Harper and wrapped his arms around her.

"She'll be okay," Zander whispered.

Jared wanted to kick Zander into action, but he thought better of it when Harper responded to the hug by stiffening her spine. If she was close to falling apart before, she thought better of it and forced herself to remain strong for Zander's sake when she realized her best friend was near tears.

"We'll find her," Harper said, her tone firm. "I won't leave this island without her."

"None of us will." Jared tugged on Harper's hand. "Come on, Heart. She's waiting for us to find her."

Jared opted for a fast pace as they picked their way down to the beach they camped on their first night. He remained hopeful – although it was dim – that Molly needed something from her tent and innocently headed to the beach because she thought it would be safe.

By the time they hit the camp, though, Jared was fairly certain that wasn't the case. The tents that remained looked limp and ragged and three of them were completely ripped apart.

"That storm was worse than we thought, huh?" Jared didn't bother faking a smile as he released Harper's hand and hunkered down so he could peer inside one of the tents. The few belongings left behind were drenched and filthy. "She's not in here."

Harper knew it was a losing proposition, but she bent down so she could look inside the next one. "She's not here either."

"We'll find her, Harper."

Harper didn't respond, instead planting her hands on her hips and turning to face the water. "Molly!" She screeched so loudly she caused Jared to jolt. He opened his mouth to chide her and then realized it wouldn't do any good and instead let her scream as much as she wanted. "Molly!"

Jared thought his heart might break due to the expression on her face. She took things to heart, especially guilt, and it was the one thing he would change about her if he could. She carried the weight of the world on her shoulders at times and he was desperate to ease her burden.

"She couldn't have gone far, Harper," Jared said, choosing his words carefully. "I'm sure she's ... ." *What? Close?* Jared had no idea if that was true. He had no idea if Molly was even alive. All he knew was that the expedition started out with three women and they were down to one. His woman. The one he loved beyond reason. "I need to get you off this island."

Jared meant to say the words to himself, but Harper snapped her head in his direction, signifying she heard them.

"I just told you that I'm not leaving this island without Molly," Harper exploded. "If you think you can bully me into leaving, you've got another think coming."

Jared held his hands up in mock surrender. "I didn't mean to say that out loud."

"You meant to think it, though."

"I did." Jared refused to back down. "You're the last woman standing and if you think I'm going to lose you then you're crazy."

"Who said anything about losing me? I have no intention of getting lost."

"I'm going to bet Molly didn't either."

The simple statement was enough to cause Harper to rear back as if she'd been slapped, her stomach rolling as she vainly fought to hold off the tears burning her eyes. Jared read her expression and hated himself for being so callous.

"Don't cry. Please don't cry." Jared moved to her, jerking her into his arms as she burst into tears. She struggled so hard to be strong even when the situation didn't warrant it that Jared couldn't help but be bowled over by her determination. "Heart, I'm sorry. I shouldn't have said that."

"I'm afraid," Harper choked out, burying her face in the hollow between Jared's neck and shoulder. "I'm afraid she's dead and we didn't even wake up when she was taken."

Jared stroked the back of her head, doing his best to soothe even though he knew it wasn't possible. "We don't know that she was taken, sweetheart. She could've walked away on her own and ... ."

"And what?" Harper challenged. "She didn't disappear on her own. She knows it would drive us crazy."

"I know." Jared held her as close as he could manage without crawling inside of her. "I'm going to do my very best to find her. I swear it."

"I know you will."

"I won't lose you, though. No matter what, you cannot separate from me for anything. Do you understand?"

Harper sniffled a bit as she lifted her tear-streaked face. "What if I have to go to the bathroom?"

"Then we'll do it together."

Harper immediately started shaking her head. "No way."

Jared adopted a firm expression. "Then you'll have to hold it."

"That's how you get bladder infections."

"Then I guess you're going to have to get used to going to the bathroom with me around," Jared charged. "I've seen everything you've got anyway. It's not a big deal."

Harper's lower lip trembled, this time for an entirely different reason. "You're mean."

"Oh, geez." Jared pinched the bridge of his nose to ward off an oncoming headache. "We'll have this argument later. We need to focus on a plan now. Maybe the others will luck out and find her wandering around the island."

"You don't really believe that," Harper argued. "Besides ... now that it's been brought up I really have to go."

"Then go."

Harper shook her head. "I would rather get a bladder infection."

"Then get a bladder infection." Jared was well aware what she was trying to do and he refused to kowtow to her whims. "You can knock those out with antibiotics, right?"

Harper narrowed her eyes to dangerous blue slits. "You can. Of course, while I'm on the antibiotics we won't be able to have sex because that could make things worse." She was totally making that up, but she internally rationalized that there was no reason Jared had to know that.

Jared responded with a growl. "We'll figure something out. In fact ... ." He didn't get a chance to finish because he heard someone yelling his name. He snapped his head to a spot farther down the beach, hoping against hope Zander and Shawn found Molly, but instead he saw Zander waving wildly as the flamboyant man tried to get his attention. "Can you go in front of Zander?"

"Not in front of him, but I can go if he's close and doesn't look."

"Then come on." Jared grabbed Harper's hand and broke into a run. Zander was far too animated to have found nothing. He didn't slow his pace until he was within hearing distance. "What is it?"

"Look!" Zander gestured toward the water.

Jared felt a sickening sensation wash over him as he calmly flicked his eyes to the water. He expected to find a body floating on the slow-moving waves – why else would Zander be so worked up, after all – but instead he saw something else entirely. "What the ... ?"

Harper followed his gaze, her eyes widening when she saw the boat bobbing on the water about five hundred feet from the beach. "Is that the boat we came out here on?"

"The Sally May," Zander confirmed, nodding.

"But how?" Jared was dumbfounded. "They left heading in the other direction."

"I don't know how, but the boat looks empty," Zander replied. "We've been calling out to them and trying to get their attention for the past five minutes. No one answers and we can't see any movement."

"Son of a ... ." Jared blew out a weary sigh. "Get the members of Michael's group. I want to talk to them."

"They're already on their way."


**JARED MANAGED TO** MAINTAIN AN AIR OF CALM UNTIL Michael, Steve, Trey, and Finn joined their small group. The façade faded quickly when Michael opened his mouth.

"It's a boat."

"Oh, really?" Sarcasm practically dripped from Jared's tongue. "It's a boat? I never would've figured that out myself. I'm just ... tickled pink ... that you noticed."

"Hey, dude, I know you're straight so you can get away with saying a lot of things, but you can't get away with that," Zander noted. "Only gay guys and old ladies can say 'tickled pink' without losing their street cred."

Jared scorched Zander with a murderous look. "Really?"

Zander correctly read Jared's mood and shook his head. "No. I was just talking to hear myself talk. Carry on."

"Great," Jared gritted out. "Yes, it's a boat, Michael. It's the boat we came out here on. It's empty as far as we can tell. Do you want to explain how that happened?"

Michael balked. "How should I know? Perhaps your guy screwed up and lost his way."

Jared didn't believe that for a second. "Eric knows how to get back to Whisper Cove."

"Maybe they came back," Finn suggested, tilting his head to the side so he could study the boat. "Maybe they reported what happened and came back to help."

"Then why is the boat out there?" Jared asked.

Finn shrugged. "Maybe it broke down."

"Then how come no one is on the boat?"

"Maybe they're down in the hold sleeping," Finn replied. "No one found any bodies, right? They probably figured no one would be up to see them until at least dawn. Hey, maybe Molly swam out there to find out what's going on."

The thought hadn't even occurred to Jared, and when he risked a look at Harper he found her mulling the same scenario.

"I don't think she would do that," Harper said finally. "Why wouldn't she wake us up instead?"

"Maybe she was excited," Trey interjected. "She clearly had a thing going on with that other guy in your group."

Harper's eyebrows flew up her forehead. "Excuse me?"

"Oh, yeah, they're totally a couple." Finn bobbed his head in agreement. "They're hiding it for some reason, though. I think the dude is the one who made that decision because the chick isn't happy."

Harper was flabbergasted ... and dubious. "But no. He has a crush on me."

Jared slid her a sidelong look. "I thought you said he was over that."

"He is, but I'm not easy to get over."

It wasn't a funny situation, but Jared couldn't stop his lips from curving. "No, and that's why I plan on keeping you for the long haul. Still ... that might explain why they've been so snippy with each other. Maybe they are hooking up. I suggested that exact thing to him when he left and he didn't deny it, although I didn't use those exact words."

Harper racked her brain for hints that was true, finally shifting her eyes to Zander. "What do you think?"

Zander held his hands palms up and shrugged. "I think that Molly had a huge crush on Eric and maybe they got drunk together and did the horizontal hula. I've always thought that would happen and then Eric would think better of it the next morning and we would ultimately have to fire one of them because the fighting would get so bad."

Harper wanted to argue with the scenario, but she couldn't. She'd often thought that might happen, too. "But we would've known if they had sex," she argued. "Neither one of them is good at hiding things."

"Why do you think they've been sniping at one another?" Trey asked.

"I ... ." Harper pressed the heel of her hand to her forehead and groaned. "Crap."

"You'd better be saying that because you think you're a bad boss for not noticing and not because you're sad about Eric getting over his crush," Jared warned, his eyes never leaving the boat. "I don't see any movement out there, but I guess they could be asleep under the deck."

"We need to find out," Shawn said. "We need to know for sure."

"We also need to know if they made it to Whisper Cove," Jared added. "I was working on the assumption that Mel was on his way out here. Eric and John might not have made it back to town, though, so that changes things."

"What if he's not on his way out here?" Zander asked, fear curling in his belly. "What if we're stuck here forever?"

"We're not going to be stuck here forever," Jared said, fighting the urge to roll his eyes. "Mel knows when we're supposed to be back and when I'm supposed to return to work. If we're not back tomorrow, he'll worry enough to send someone out here."

Zander was mollified. "Especially because I'm his favorite nephew."

"Yeah, he mentions that all of the time," Jared drawled, his eyes fixed on the boat. "I need to swim out there."

"The water is going to be cold," Harper argued. "You might get sick."

"I won't get sick, but someone needs to look at that boat," Jared said. "I think that means I'm the one who has to swim out there."

"You're not going alone," Shawn argued, reaching for his shirt. "I'll go with you."

"Wait a second." Harper wasn't happy with the situation. "I don't want you going out there alone."

Jared flashed a patient smile. "That's why Shawn is going with me. I'll be fine. I won't be but a half hour at the most. If I find the others there, we'll all swim back together."

Harper darted a look at Zander to see what he was thinking. "Are you okay with this?"

"I don't know," Zander replied, his expression serious. "I don't think Jared should go alone, though, so I guess I have to be."

"That doesn't mean you should be separated from Shawn." Harper made up her mind on the spot. "I'll swim out there with Jared."

Jared immediately started shaking his head. "Absolutely not."

"Why?"

"Because the water is cold."

"You said it wasn't that bad."

"Yeah, well ... no."

Harper crossed her arms over her chest, her stubbornness coming out to play. "I want one good reason why that has nothing to do with me not having a penis."

"I ... ." Jared worked his jaw as he tried to think of a reason. Finally he could do nothing but shake his head. "Fine. If you get a cold, though, I'm going to force you into bed for a week and make you eat chicken noodle soup and take constant baths with me."

"I think you're supposed to come up with a punishment instead of a reward in situations like this, dude," Shawn noted.

Zander nodded sagely. "Those are both things she likes."

Jared rolled his eyes. "Fine. Then I'll make you go to the bathroom in front of me, Heart. How does that sound?"

"Like some really kinky thing none of us what to be involved in," Trey replied, grinning when he saw the dark look on Jared's face. "What? I'm just trying to lighten the mood."

"Whatever." Jared heaved out a sigh as he looked Harper up and down. "I have my boxer shorts. What are you going to swim in?"

"I'm wearing a sports bra and boy shorts," Harper replied. "It's just like a bathing suit. In fact, it covers more than my bathing suit."

Jared took on a wistful expression as he remembered a certain beach day over the summer, and the itsy-bitsy bikini she wore to enjoy it. "I really miss hammocking."

Harper snorted a laugh as she reached for her shirt. "Come on. I need to know what's out there."

Jared followed suit. "Okay, but you do what I say when we reach the boat. Do you understand?"

Harper mock saluted. "Yes, sir."

"Oh, that's hot," Trey intoned.

Jared extended a warning finger. "Turn around."

Trey chuckled. "Do you really think I'm going to ogle your girl-friend or something?"

"Turn around or I will thump you," Jared seethed. "I'm not kidding."

"Wow. You guys are absolutely no fun." Trey turned his back as Harper disrobed, crossing his arms over his chest. "I can't wait for this job to be done."

"I think we all agree with that," Jared said. "All I want is my girl and off this island. It can't happen fast enough."

## 15

# FIFTEEN

Harper gritted her teeth as she waded into the water. She insisted on being the one to accompany Jared so there was no way she would complain about the temperature. She stroked out quickly, her muscle memory taking over as she valiantly tried to keep her mind busy. Thankfully the boat wasn't far away so it wouldn't take them long to get to it.

Jared watched her out of the corner of his eye, internally chuckling at the way she clenched her jaw. She was freezing but would never admit to it. That wasn't her way. She was far too stubborn. Sometimes he found the trait annoying. Other times he found it endearing. This was an example of the latter. He hadn't been keen on leaving her even though he knew Zander would protect Harper with his life. Now he didn't have to make the choice.

They reached the boat at the same time. On a normal day, Jared would've considered himself a gentleman and hoisted Harper up on the ladder ahead of him. He was too worried what he would find onboard, though, and swung onto the ladder before she could.

"Follow me but be ready to jump back in the water in case we find something bad."

Harper mutely nodded. She had an inkling what the "something bad" Jared worried about was. Thankfully for both of them, when they reached the top of the ladder they found it completely empty.

"Anything?" Harper furrowed her brow as she glanced around.

"No sign of anyone," Jared replied, rubbing his hand over her cold skin. "Stay here a second." He disappeared beneath the deck to scan the small cabin below but was back within less than a minute. "Empty."

Harper swallowed hard. "Any signs of a struggle?"

"No. It's just empty." Jared exhaled heavily through his nose and moved to the boat controls, frowning when he found the ignition empty. "The keys are gone."

Harper considered herself fairly intuitive, but she had no idea what that meant. "What do you think happened?"

"I think someone took the keys."

"I figured that out myself," Harper said dryly. "Why would they do that?"

"I have no idea," Jared answered. "There are a couple of theories that fit the scenario."

"What are they?"

Jared noticed Harper shivering and tugged her to him so he could share some of his body heat. He was nowhere near as cold as he thought he would be, but she appeared to be suffering greatly.

"The first is that Eric and John made it to Whisper Cove, alerted Mel to what was going on, and decided to head back to the island despite the storm," Jared explained. "They wouldn't have been able to get too close to the island due to the waves so they dropped anchor and swam in."

"So where are they?"

"I have no idea. Under that scenario, they met with trouble before they got to us. Maybe the ghosts didn't bother us because they were busy with John and Eric."

"And what happened to Molly under that scenario?" Harper pressed. "How do you explain her disappearance?"

"Heart, I don't know. None of the scenarios plug every plot hole. They're merely a jumping off point."

"What is your other scenario?"

"Someone knew that they were out here and waited for them on the beach, perhaps even enticing them to swim in somehow," Jared replied. "I'm not sure how they knew ... maybe they heard something we didn't and came out to investigate."

"And then what?" Harper asked. "Whoever it was killed them?"

"Or took them captive."

"To what end?"

"I don't know." Jared figured Harper was tired of hearing that answer, but he didn't have another one to give her. "I think that we need to seriously consider the fact that not everything happening right now is ghost related, though."

Harper dug her fingers into Jared's flank. "You think we have someone dangerous with us, don't you?"

"I think that's the only answer that makes any sense," Jared replied. "I think it's entirely possible that Lucy walked off to force your hand. That doesn't explain why she's still missing, though."

"That doesn't mean the ghosts didn't do something to her."

"What?" Jared pulled back slightly. "What could they do to her? I'm not being difficult. I really want to know."

"Ghosts can affect the physical world," Harper reminded him. "The last ghost Zander and I took down hurled apples at us."

"Yes, you smelled like an odd little pie."

"Ha, ha." Harper tapped her finger against his chest. "Ghosts can hurt humans if they have enough energy behind them. The ghosts at the asylum have a lot of rage fueling them, maybe a little mental illness, and a whole lot of isolation, so they have a lot of anger to get out."

"Do you think it's possible for a ghost to kidnap someone? I'm talking about taking them without us knowing and keeping them captive."

Harper tilted her head to the side, considering. "Yes. I don't know how probable it is, but I do think it's possible."

"Okay, where would a ghost be able to keep someone that wouldn't be easy to mount an escape?"

"Hmm. Good question. You're using your brain." Harper flicked

Jared's ear as she thought. "We looked over the plans last night. Did anything stick out to you?"

"Apparently you have a better construction brain than me because none of it looked odd to me. You have better instincts for this stuff. What do you think?"

"I think that we need to look at it logically," Harper replied. "They needed lockdown wards, right? They had legitimate mentally disturbed individuals here. That means they needed to be able to lock some of the wards for their own security."

"That makes a lot of sense, Heart."

"It also means we've been looking in the wrong place from the start," Harper pointed out. "I was afraid of the basement because a lot of terrible things happened there. The rooms are on the second floor, though. I'm sure equally terrible things happened there and that was the place the souls called home at the time of their deaths."

Jared caught on to what she was saying. "So ... upstairs?"

Harper nodded her head. "Upstairs. It's the only logical place to look next."

"Then let's get going." Jared cast one more glance around the boat and shook his head. "The anchor is down. The boat isn't going anywhere. Hopefully we'll be able to find the keys."

"If we find Molly and the keys, I want to get out of here," Harper said. "We can send someone back for Lucy and the others."

"What about Eric?"

Harper chewed on her bottom lip. "I want Eric, too, but we have no idea if he's even on the island. He could be back in Whisper Cove for all we know. Maybe he told Mel what was happening and stayed behind and John came back on his own."

"That's definitely another possibility," Jared conceded. "If Molly and Eric were involved, though – even if it was going wrong – I don't think he's the type of guy who would leave her to fend for herself. I also don't think he's the type of guy who would leave you and Zander. He would happily leave me."

"He would." Harper cracked a wan smile. "Maybe he stayed behind to ride on a different boat with Mel, though. I can see him doing that."

"I can, too." Jared rubbed the top of his head as blew out a heavy breath. "We don't have nearly enough evidence. I don't know what to make out of any of this."

"The only thing we know for sure is that someone from their team probably has to be involved," Harper said. "That means, once we get back to shore, we need to stay with Shawn and Zander no matter what. No more splitting up."

"No more splitting up," Jared agreed. "There are only four of us now. We have to remain together."

"Both groups are down two people," Harper mused. "We've lost Eric and Molly. They've lost Lucy and John. Do you think that's on purpose?"

"I don't know. I know I don't like the fact that two women appear to have been kidnapped. You're sticking close to me no matter what. I don't care how quirky you are about going to the bathroom in front of me."

"I went while we were swimming." Harper was sheepish. "I couldn't help myself."

Jared snorted. "I'm fine with that. You're going to have to get over going on land, though. I'm not taking you swimming whenever you have to go."

"I'll just stop drinking liquids."

Jared sighed, resigned. "We'll figure it out. Now, come on. We need to get back to the island. Once there, we're sticking close as a foursome."

"And then we're heading to the second floor," Harper said. "I think that's our best bet."

"I think that's the only move that makes sense," Jared agreed. "Let's go."


**JARED CALMLY REPORTED** WHAT THEY FOUND ON THE boat while Shawn and Zander served as human shields to protect Harper while she changed out of her wet clothes. She didn't have anything fresh so she hopped into the clothes she discarded on the beach and went commando, something that made Jared's mind wander when it should be focused on other things.

Zander fixed an easy meal of lunchmeat sandwiches, refusing to waste time on anything gourmet, and then Jared explained what would happen next.

"We're going to the second floor."

Michael balked. "I think we should go back to the basement."

"You only think that because you heard me say that the truly bad things happened in the basement," Harper countered, leaning back so Zander could fuss with her hair. "You're still worried about getting good footage for your show. We're worried about far more important things."

"Speaking of that, if you have a hand in the two members of our group going missing, I'll charge you," Jared warned. "Not only will I do that, but I'll confiscate your footage and make sure it never sees the light of day."

"You can't do that!" Michael was incensed. "That's my property."

"You would be surprised at what I'm capable of doing," Jared shot back. "This is not a laughing matter to us. That boat was empty and the keys were gone. That means someone took the keys for a reason."

"And what reason would that be?" Finn asked.

"I honestly have no idea," Jared replied. "Finding Eric and Molly is the only thing we're concerned about at this time. If you get in our way, if you impede our progress, you're not going to like what happens."

"And what's that?" Steve asked. He'd been oddly quiet since the discovery of Molly's disappearance two hours before.

"Let's just say it will be ugly and leave it at that," Jared said. "Now, we're going upstairs. We searched the basement and found nothing. If our people are still alive, that means they're being kept somewhere. Harper had a good idea about that."

"I'm sure she did," Trey said dryly. "You seem to think all of her ideas are good."

"That's because she knows what she's doing and is my little genius."

"She knows what she's doing with ghosts," Trey pressed. "As far as I can tell, we're not dealing with ghosts. We're dealing with an abandoned asylum and a bunch of hysterics."

Jared gritted his teeth to keep from exploding, sucking in a long breath to calm himself. "Harper saw Anna Pritchard and talked to her. Anna said the place was crawling with spirits. What more do you want?"

"I would like someone else to have seen a ghost," Trey replied without hesitation. "I find it convenient that she only found one ghost to talk to and it just happened to be off camera."

"I find that suspicious, too," Michael added. "I'm starting to think she's a fraud. We didn't so much as hear a peep last night."

"And yet Molly is missing," Zander argued, his hackles rising. "She didn't just get up in the middle of the night and decide to play a prank on us."

"She has green hair," Finn argued. "I don't think that speaks to how diligent an employee she is."

"What does it matter what color her hair is?" Shawn asked, defensive on Molly's behalf. "She's a young girl who never seeks out trouble. If you've done something to her ... ."

"If anyone here has done something to her I'll make sure they're locked up for the rest of their lives," Jared interjected, his eyes dark and dangerous. "I've had just about enough of you people."

"Oh, well, color me shocked," Trey intoned. "Would you like us to get to our knees and grovel for your forgiveness now, or wait until you've verbally abused us a bit more?"

Jared, his hands clenched into fists as his sides, took a furious step in Trey's direction. Harper stopped him with a hand to his arm.

"Don't bother, Jared. He's not worth it."

Jared pinned Harper with a gaze, saw the worry flitting through the fathomless depths of her blue eyes, and purposely vented some of the anger fueling him. "He's not. It's okay." He cupped the back of her head and pressed a quick kiss to her forehead. "We're going to find Molly right now."

"And what about us?" Michael asked, irritation evident. "We're still filming a television show."

"I don't really care what you do," Jared replied. "Quite frankly, I can't help being suspicious about a group of men who aren't even a little bit worried about the fact that two young women have gone missing."

"They're probably just wandering around," Finn protested. "They're playing a game. That's what women do."

"I can't speak for what Lucy does in her spare time, but that's not what Molly does," Jared snapped. "Either way, I don't care what you do. We're going upstairs to find our friends. You guys can sit here and stroke each other's egos until night falls again for all I care."

"Night? You think we're going to have to spend another night here?" Michael blanched. "We were originally supposed to go home tomorrow morning, but I assumed we would leave this afternoon given the ... shift ... in the focus of this episode."

"We're not in an episode of television," Jared pointed out. "We're stuck on an island and four people are unaccounted for. Now, there's a possibility that Eric and John made it to Whisper Cove and got help. I'm not holding my breath for that, though, because I think Mel would already be here if they had."

"So, what? Do you think they're dead or something?" Michael's expression told Jared exactly what the producer thought of the possibility.

"I certainly hope not," Jared said. "I'm not sitting around and waiting for something to happen, though. We need to find our people. If we find yours in the process, so much the better. We can't sit around and hope for the best, though. We have to be proactive."

"And we certainly can't sit around waiting for something to happen so you can make a fun television show," Harper added. "We're done playing by your rules. We're playing by our own rules."

"Yay!" Zander pumped his fist. "You can bite us."

Trey rolled his eyes. "I don't see how you guys get any work done when you act the way you do. Of course, you probably don't do real work. You're the same as the other ghost hunters we've come across over the years. You're all frauds."

"All of our ghost hunters have been legitimate," Michael argued. "We put that right on the front crawl of each episode."

Trey made a disgusted sound in the back of his throat. "Whatever."

"It's true," Michael snapped. "Ms. Harlow might not be real – and I'm beginning to seriously doubt her credentials, she's obviously fooled a lot of people who don't know better – but everyone else has been one hundred percent authentic."

"Hey!" Zander was affronted on Harper's behalf. "Harp is the real deal. You're the frauds."

"Don't bother." Harper waved off Zander's righteous indignation. "They're idiots, Zander. I didn't even want to be on this stupid show."

"Then why did you agree?" Michael challenged.

"Because Zander wanted it and I love Zander," Harper replied, unruffled by the producer's tone. "Also ... I always wanted to see this place. I thought I would regret it if I didn't come. Now I've seen it, though. I want to find Molly and Eric, help Anna, and get out of here."

"Well, that's convenient," Trey said. "You'll cash your paycheck, won't you?"

"You'd better hope that Molly and Eric are alive," Jared interjected, linking his fingers with Harper's. "If they're not, you're going to have a lot more to worry about than a paycheck. Guys, grab your flashlights and extra batteries. We're going to the second floor."

He led the small group toward the stairs. "If you guys know what's good for you, you'll start looking, too," he added. "The sooner all of our team members are accounted for, the sooner we'll have answers."

"And what answers do you expect to find?" Finn asked.

Jared shrugged, noncommittal. "I'm not sure yet, but I am sure that not everything is as it seems. Something else is going on here, and I'm going to find out exactly what that is. I can promise you that."

## ✤ 16 ✤

## SIXTEEN

"I want eyes on Harper at all times," Jared announced, keeping his gaze on the stairs as they ascended to the second floor. He didn't want to risk accidentally stepping on a weak part of the floor and falling through so he was hyper-vigilant when scanning the fragile boards. "That means she doesn't go anywhere alone. That includes the bathroom, no matter how much she whines."

"You know I can hear you, right?" Harper drawled. "I've not been rendered suddenly deaf or dumb."

"I never thought you were." Jared squeezed her hand. "I was saying it because you're going to be the difficult one. Shawn and Zander are already on board with the plan."

Harper slowed her pace. "Excuse me. I am not a child. I am more than capable of taking care of myself."

"Under normal circumstances, I would agree," Jared said. "These aren't normal circumstances. We're in a contained environment, Heart. Do you know what that means?"

"Apparently that you're going to talk down to me for the next ten minutes." Harper jerked her hand away from Jared and crossed her arms over her chest as she shifted her attention from her boyfriend's handsome face to the faded artwork on the wall. "I can't wait for this."

"I am not talking down to you," Jared argued. "I'm freaking out because I want to keep the woman I love safe."

Harper's expression softened. "I should be angry at you for manipulating me that way."

Jared's lips curved. "I can live with you being angry. I cannot live with losing you. Do you understand? You have to stay with us at all times. This isn't a game."

"I know it's not a game." Harper instinctively grabbed his fingers and squeezed a bit harder than necessary to get her point across. She was agitated with his bossy nature, but she understood where he was coming from. "I'm not trying to mess around or anything. It's just ... I don't think that being on top of each other is going to be healthy for our relationship."

Zander opened his mouth, something filthy on his tongue, but Jared flicked the side of his head to keep him quiet.

"You can let some of them go," Jared chided before fixing his full attention on Harper. "As for our relationship, I choose to believe it will survive this. If it doesn't, I will not be happy. I will not let anything happen to you, though. I refuse. So ... if you feel that's grounds to break up with me, I guess I can't stop you."

Harper's eyes flashed with indignation. "That's not what I meant and you know it."

"Oh, I know." Jared bobbed his head in understanding. "You were trying to manipulate me into letting you go to the bathroom by yourself. It's not going to happen."

"But ... ."

"No." Jared's voice was icy. "I will not lose you." He almost broke but managed to hold it together, for her sake as well as his.

"Harp, you're torturing him," Zander announced, taking everyone by surprise when he landed on Jared's side of the argument. "Do you want to torture him? I don't think you do. I think you're just a bit set in your ways when it comes to certain things. You're going to have to let that go, though."

Harper vigorously rubbed her cheeks to get the circulation going. "Fine," she huffed out. "I'll do what you want."

"Thank you." Jared kissed her forehead. "We'll figure out a way for you to keep your prudish streak alive and make sure I don't have to be away from you. I promise."

Harper made an exaggerated face. "I do not have a prudish streak."

Jared, Zander, and Shawn snorted in unison, which only served to make the situation worse.

"I'm not prudish," Harper snapped.

"You're lovely, sweet, and kind," Jared offered, lifting his flashlight a bit when they hit the top of the stairs. "The prudish streak is actually kind of cute when we're not fighting off ghosts and potential murderers."

"I think so, too." Shawn winked at Harper.

"I hate the prudish streak, but you wouldn't be you without it and I love you," Zander said, moving closer to Harper's back as he peered over her shoulder. "Which way, Harp?"

That was a good question. Harper narrowed her eyes as her gaze bounced from the left to the right. She tried to picture the plans they scanned from the night before and hesitantly extended her finger to point toward the right. "I think we should go that way."

Jared knew better than asking why. "Okay. Everyone stick close together, and be on the lookout in case anyone from the other group decides to follow us."

"Why is that something to worry about?" Shawn asked, legitimately curious.

Jared spared a glance for Harper before plowing forward. "We didn't say anything downstairs because we didn't want to alert anyone to what we suspected, but we believe we're in trouble from a human force."

"So we're not dealing with ghosts?" Shawn furrowed his brow. "How does that work?"

"Oh, I think we're dealing with ghosts, but I don't think they had anything to do with what happened on that boat," Jared replied, allowing Harper to take her time as they moved into a dark hallway. "Go slow," he whispered, flicking his flashlight beam to his left. "Watch the floor very closely."

Shawn kept his beam on the floor as Zander and Jared searched the hallway walls. Harper kept her gaze straight forward, her pace slowing to a delayed shuffle before completely stopping. Shawn was the first to notice.

"What is it, Harper?"

Jared jerked his head to the right and scanned her profile. He recognized the rigid set of her shoulders right away. "She sees something."

"What do you see?" Zander asked.

Harper ignored them, instead focusing on the billowing presence floating in the middle of the hallway about twenty feet away. "Hello."

The ghost, a pretty woman with long, flowing curls, offered up a hint of a smile as she surveyed the small group. "Greetings." Her voice was low and gravelly, but she didn't appear dangerous.

"I'm Harper and these are my friends Jared, Zander, and Shawn."

The ghost rested her gaze on the three men before turning back to Harper. "You're not supposed to have men in the women's ward," she said, lowering her voice. "You'll get in trouble with Nurse Stinson if you're not careful."

Harper arched an eyebrow. The woman talked as if the asylum remained open, as if she still lived by the same rules she did in life. Harper theorized that it was entirely possible the woman didn't realize she was dead or that things had changed. If she'd been mentally ill in life, she very well could be the same in death.

"I promise not to incur Nurse Stinson's wrath," Harper said, her lips curving. "My friends will be quiet. Won't you?"

Jared nodded, solemn. "Of course."

The ghost giggled at his somber expression. "He's cute. Is he yours?"

That was an interesting way to phrase it and Harper wasn't sure how to answer. "He's not my property but ... yes, he's mine."

Jared's smirk reflected a mixture of amusement and love, but he wisely remained quiet.

"What about the other two?"

"Oh, well ... ." Harper wasn't sure how to answer. "They're my brothers," she said finally, earning a dark look from Zander. "We're all going to hang out in my room."

"That's not allowed." The ghost shook her head, stern. "Nurse Stinson will punish you."

Harper had no doubt that Nurse Stinson – whoever she was – probably had a sadistic streak a mile wide. "Is Nurse Stinson even here? I haven't seen her in quite some time."

"I ... ." The ghost broke off, tapping her bottom lip. "I don't know. I can look for her."

Harper wasn't keen on sending the spirit off on a wild goose chase, but she needed time to search the floor without having to answer an endless series of questions. "That would be great." Harper waited until she was gone before flicking her eyes back to Jared. "I'm going to want to put her to rest before we go, too."

"We'll see how things play out," Jared cautioned. "We might have to leave as a group – depending on what happens with Molly and Eric – and then come back when it's just us so you can do that. I'll figure out a way to make it happen. I promise. It's just ... ."

"Molly and Eric are our priority," Harper finished. "I know. We have to find them."

"So let's look around." Jared squeezed her hand before releasing it. "I'm trusting you to be very careful up here and not wander away from me."

Harper barely managed to withhold an eye roll. "I heard you the first time, Dad."

Jared pretended he didn't hear the tone. "If you keep calling me that, I will spank you when we get out of this."

"She may be a prude, but she'll probably like that," Zander noted.

Harper ignored both of them and moved down the center of the hallway. Despite her earlier bravado, she was very careful not to drift too far from her friends. It wasn't just fear for her own safety propelling her. She had no doubt Jared would be forever plagued with doubt and insecurity if he somehow lost her. He would never get over it.

"Look at this." Harper knelt down and held her flashlight over a spot on the floor. Jared moved to her side and followed her gaze, frowning when he saw the huge footprint in the center of the dust accumulated there.

"That's interesting," Jared muttered, lifting his phone and snapping a photograph of the footprint. The service on his phone didn't work, but he still had a bit of battery life left, although it wasn't much. "That means someone was up here."

"Michael and the others could've easily searched this level," Zander pointed out. "Wasn't that part of the plan yesterday? They said they were up here."

Jared shrugged. "They said they were up here, but only briefly before giving up. I took that to mean that they stood at the top of the stairs and yelled for Lucy. I don't think they did a very thorough search."

"They also could've broken off during the afternoon without us noticing," Harper said. "We spent a lot of time yesterday going over the map. We were in the registry office for a long time, too. They were very bored with that part of the day."

"Then we spent a few hours going over the files Harper found once we couldn't find Lucy in the basement," Jared added. "I wasn't paying attention to what they were doing while that was going on because I was trying to decide if Lucy took off on her own or was taken."

"I still think she took off on purpose," Harper said, tilting her head to the side. "I think she was trying to make a very special episode of television. I simply think she ran into trouble once she separated."

"Of the human or paranormal kind?" Shawn asked.

"That is the question, isn't it?" Harper wiggled her eyebrows as she stood. "I wish Anna was around. We need help and I want to ask someone who seems relatively normal because we don't have a lot of time to waste."

"Can you call her?" Jared asked.

"She's not a dog."

"No, but she seemed eager to talk to you before."

Harper couldn't argue with that so she planted her hands on her hips, blew out a sigh, and nodded. "I can try." She lifted her chin and raised her voice. "Anna?" Harper's voice sounded eerie as it echoed down the hallway. She didn't appear right away. "Anna? Can you please come talk to us?"

Harper let her flashlight drift up and down the hallway as she looked for signs of Anna Pritchard. At one point, when she opened her mouth to yell for a third time, a gaunt-looking ghost in a nightgown popped into being in front of Harper and held a ghostly finger to her lips.

"Shh!"

Harper was so surprised that she stumbled backward, smacking into Jared's broad chest as he brought an arm around her in a protective fashion.

"What is it?"

"The second floor is definitely more active than the basement," Harper replied, working overtime to calm herself. "It's probably because they associate the wards with being home, but I would've thought that they would spread out over the years. I just don't get it."

"That's because you can't see the entire picture," Anna announced, blinking into existence less than a foot in front of Harper's face and causing the ghost hunter to yelp as she smacked into Jared. "I think you will soon, but it's not an easy process to live with."

"Harper." Jared clutched his blonde to his chest. He was working at a disadvantage because he couldn't see what threatened her. It frustrated him to no end ... and made him antsy. "What is it, Heart?"

"Anna," Harper squeaked out, sucking in gaping mouthfuls of oxygen as she tried to calm herself. "She's here."

"Okay." Jared slid his arm around Harper's waist to keep her close. "What does she say?"

"So far she's essentially said 'hello' and then added something cryptic about me getting the full picture eventually," Harper replied, recovering a bit. "Now ... shh. Let me talk to Anna for a second."

Anna's smile was serene as her gaze bounced between faces. "You're surrounded by handsome men. Will you marry one of them?"

"Maybe," Harper hedged, uncomfortable.

"I'm assuming that one is your best prospect." Anna inclined her chin in Jared's direction. "He's very handsome."

"He knows that," Harper said dryly.

"The other two are handsome, too." Anna smiled at Zander. "Especially this one."

Harper couldn't stop herself from snickering. "He knows that, too."

Harper poked Zander's side. "Anna thinks you're handsome. Actually, she thinks all of you are handsome."

"We do our best," Jared said. "Ask her if she's seen any activity up here."

Harper shot him a quelling look. "I've got it."

"I'm starting to see what you meant by all of this time on top of each other affecting our relationship," Jared muttered under his breath. "I kind of want to muzzle you a little bit."

"I heard that," Harper snapped, ignoring the way he rolled his eyes and smiling for Anna's benefit. "Do you spend most of your time up here?"

"I travel all over the facility," Anna replied. "I'm not limited by the rules. Others are ... confused ... about what is and what is not allowed."

That made sense to Harper in an odd sort of way. "Have you been watching us since we talked yesterday?"

"I have checked in on occasion," Anna confirmed. "I was very interested in this one cooking chicken in a fireplace. Everyone seemed to like it, though, so it went better than expected."

Harper snickered. "He's a good cook. I wasn't surprised the chicken turned out so well."

Zander preened when he realized they were talking about him. "I'm an awesome cook. I'm the best cook in the world. In fact, I should give lessons I'm such a good cook."

"He's also humble." Anna's eyes lit with mirth as she swirled. "What is it you want to know, Harper Harlow? I'm surprised you remain on the property."

"We've had a few issues," Harper hedged. "A few members of our team are missing."

"I noticed." Anna looked sympathetic. "Will you stay until you find them?"

"Yes." Harper answered without hesitation. "I won't leave without Molly. Do you know where she is?"

Anna looked uncomfortable with the question. "No, but I might be able to find out. Is that what you wish?"

Harper nodded. "I need to find her. We're also looking for the woman who disappeared yesterday and two men who were on a boat. I don't suppose you know where any of them are, do you?"

"The two women are probably together, but I can't confirm that as I haven't actually seen them. It's just an inkling," Anna replied. "As for the men, is one of them hurt?"

The question caught Harper off guard. "I don't know. We didn't see signs of struggle on the boat or anything, but I think it's possible that one of them is hurt. Why? Have you seen someone who is hurt?"

"Yes."

Harper's breath caught in her throat. "Is he close?"

"He's very close." Anna turned and floated down the hallway. "He's also extremely ill. Will you fix him?"

"I certainly hope so," Harper replied, increasing her pace as she followed Anna. "Do you know who it is? What does he look like?"

Anna didn't immediately answer, instead pointing toward a closed door that boasted a rocking horse over the frame. Harper lifted her eyes, realization dawning. "This is the children's ward, isn't it?"

"Yes," Anna confirmed. "One of your missing friends is inside. I'm not sure which one ... or if he can be helped."

Harper swallowed hard. "I guess we're about to find out."

Since he only heard one side of the conversation, Jared was confused when Harper reached for the handle. "What are you doing?"

Harper ignored him and lifted her flashlight as the door swung open, a small cry escaping her throat when she saw a head pop up from one of the beds and meet her gaze, glazed eyes expressing confusion and relief.

"Harper?"

"Omigod, it's Eric!" Harper bolted into the room. "He's alive."

"Of course I'm alive," Eric muttered, resting his head on the small bed as he stared at the ceiling. "How long I'll be alive is another question entirely."

## ❧ 17 ❧

# SEVENTEEN

arper was the first to make it to Eric's side. In the limited light, she couldn't see where he was hurt, but his face was covered with a thin sheen of sweat.

"What's wrong?"

"I believe everything is wrong," Eric gritted out. "Where would you like to start?"

Jared lifted his flashlight and focused the beam on Eric's face, causing him to groan as he pressed his eyes shut and slung an arm over his face as a blocking mechanism. "We need more light."

"Hold on." Shawn moved to the window on the far side of the room and tugged on the heavy drapes. They didn't move, but that didn't dissuade Shawn from trying again. This time the drapes gave way, ripping from the rod and falling to the ground in a heap. The light that spilled into the room thanks to the sunshine on the other side of the dirty window was a welcome sight.

"That's better, huh?" Harper forced a smile as she switched off her flashlight and rested a hand on Eric's shoulder. "How did you get here?"

"That's a very interesting question," Eric muttered. "I'm not quite sure. Everything is a jumble."

"I led him here," Anna supplied, causing Harper to stare at the ghost. She was more transparent due to the light, but Harper could still make out the bulk of her features.

"You led him here?" Harper was understandably surprised. "How?"

"He was outside," Anna replied. "He was confused and had trouble standing. I coaxed him in to get him out of the elements."

"Do you remember that?" Harper asked Eric.

"Remember what?" Eric asked, his voice weak. "I can't hear her. You're the only one who can."

"She said she led you inside," Harper prodded. "Was this last night?"

Anna nodded. "It was dark."

"I don't know." Eric's expression was pained. "Everything is fuzzy."

"Tell me what you do remember," Jared prodded, kneeling next to Harper and gently running his hands over the back of Eric's head. "You have a knot here. I think you hit your head." He flashed his light in Eric's eyes again, ignoring the way the other man protested. "I'm not a doctor, but I think you have a concussion."

"That would explain the pounding in my head," Eric muttered. "As for what I remember, it's all kind of murky."

"Did you make it to Whisper Cove?" Zander asked hopefully. "Is Uncle Mel on his way?"

"We didn't make it to Whisper Cove," Eric replied. "The weather changed. We were closer to the island than town. We thought we would be safe if we marked our progress by returning to the island and then setting out again after the storm passed. Neither one of us was very good with the equipment."

"I was afraid of that," Jared muttered. "I wouldn't be good with it either. I'm not much of a boat person."

"So what happened?" Shawn prodded. "You came back to the island and ... what?"

"It was a rocky wait," Eric explained. "We dropped anchor so we wouldn't drift, but the boat was up and down so much that I got sick." He was chagrined to admit it. "We had to take cover below deck and I spent the entire time throwing up in a bucket."

"Then what happened?" Jared asked.

"I kind of lost track of time for a bit," Eric admitted. "The storm eventually slowed enough for John to go above deck. He was hoping to get your attention on the beach."

"We weren't on the beach," Harper said. "We had to take cover inside."

"That makes sense." Eric rubbed the tender spot between his eyebrows. "That storm was something else."

"Go back to the boat." Jared's tone was gentle but firm. "You were downstairs throwing up and John went to the deck. What happened after that?"

"I have no idea," Eric replied. "I slept a bit, but he never came back. When I was finally feeling well enough to stand, I went upstairs and he wasn't on the boat. He was just ... gone."

"Gone?" Harper's eyebrows winged up. "Do you think he tried to swim to the island?"

"That was my initial guess," Eric supplied. "I waited for him for a few hours, but I didn't hear anything on the island or in the water so I decided to head that way, too. I figured the boat would be safe because it wasn't very far offshore."

"No," Jared agreed. "Did you take the boat keys?"

"I did." Eric dug in his pocket and came up with the item in question. "I don't know why, but it didn't seem like a good idea to leave the key in the ignition so I grabbed it." He handed it to Jared. "I didn't want to risk them leaving us. I had no real proof they would do that, mind you, but I wanted to make sure it wouldn't happen."

"You did good," Jared said, exhaling heavily as he pocketed the key. "You did really good. You still haven't told us how you got injured, though."

"The water was cold and the storm, while dissipating, wasn't completely gone," Eric supplied. "It took me longer than I thought it would to get to the shore, and when I did, I was exhausted.

"I sat on the beach to rest for a minute," he continued. "I figured you guys were inside, and while I wasn't thrilled at the idea of going into the asylum at night, I guessed you were right in the main foyer."

"We were," Harper pressed her hand to Eric's forehead. He didn't seem to have a fever, but he was clearly struggling.

"I don't know how long I was out there, but I don't think it was very long," Eric said. "I heard something and looked over my shoulder, but by then it was already too late. There was a shadow and ... then next thing I knew I was on the sand and really confused."

"Someone hit you from behind," Jared murmured, rubbing the back of his neck as he tilted his head. "Do you think it was John?"

"I don't know. I honestly can't say that with any degree of certainty. I jumped to that conclusion last night but ... I didn't see him. For all I know, John could've been attacked, too. He could've been left for dead on the beach."

"We searched the beach this morning," Zander offered. "We saw the boat and realized you were back. Harper and Jared swam out there, but it was empty."

"And we couldn't figure out what happened," Jared added. "At least now we know you didn't make it back to Whisper Cove. We're on our own for at least another night. Mel should realize something is wrong when we don't come back. How long he'll wait to come looking for us is the question."

"He won't wait long," Zander said. "He loves me too much."

Jared rolled his eyes. "Let's hope so. Eric is our other concern. We need to keep him quiet. He can't be traipsing all over the asylum in his condition."

"I still don't understand how he ended up here," Shawn said, his hand gentle as he wiped the sweat from Eric's brow. "He can't see ghosts and yet Harper's ghost said she led him up here. How come?"

"That's a good question," Harper mused, turning to Anna. "Why did you lead him up here?"

"He looked injured and I wasn't sure who did it," Anna replied. "He was very ... confused. He slipped between two worlds."

"He slipped between two worlds?" Harper had a very vague idea what that meant. "Are you saying he was drifting between consciousness so you managed to make him see you when he was more open to the second sight?"

"I don't know. Perhaps." Anna did her best approximation of a shrug.

"How come you didn't lead him to us?"

"Because I was unsure who injured him," Anna replied. "I thought he would be safer up here."

Harper turned so she could study the room. "This is the children's ward, isn't it?"

"Yes."

"Did you have a lot of children here?"

"Very few. The ones that were here were ... damaged."

"Damaged how?" Harper shuffled closer to one of the empty beds and bent over, retrieving a misshapen lump of wood that resembled a long-forgotten toy. The children's ward wasn't exactly clean, but it wasn't nearly as ravaged as other parts of the asylum.

"They were examples of individuals who really needed to be here," Anna answered. "They were lost in their own heads. One was even violent."

"Violent?"

"He stabbed one of the nurses with a needle and she almost died."

"It wasn't Nurse Stinson, was it?"

Anna chuckled, the sound low and throaty. "It was. How do you know that name?"

"One of your fellow ghost refugees warned us not to be loud in the hallway," Harper replied. "She said that Nurse Stinson wouldn't like it."

"Probably Jessica," Anna supplied. "She was always terrified of Nurse Stinson."

"And how did Jessica die?"

"Badly."

Harper tilted her head to the side and fixed her full attention on Anna. "I don't suppose you remember how you died, do you?"

"No. I don't want to remember."

To Harper, that indicated Anna probably did know what happened to her, but she was uncomfortable sharing the details with others. That was certainly her right, but Harper couldn't help being curious. Instead of pressing Anna on the issue, though, she shifted back to the topic of the children's ward.

"From everything I've read, no children ever went missing here," Harper said. "How were they treated?"

"Better in some respects ... and worse in others," Anna answered. "It was a very long time ago."

Jared did his best to remain patient throughout the discussion, but he was perilously close to losing it. "Harper, I know you're interested in this stuff and I promise to sit here and let you have a long conversation with Anna when the situation warrants it, but we need to focus on the here and now."

Harper knew he was right, but that didn't stop her from chafing a bit under his directive. "I'm working on it."

"Work faster."

"I do kind of remember hearing a voice last night," Eric supplied. "It was a woman. I thought it might be Molly at first so I followed. I'm not sure how I ended up here, though. Wouldn't I have walked right past you guys? Even if you were sleeping, it seems as if one of you would've woken and noticed me."

"That's true," Shawn said. "So how did you get inside without that happening?"

"There's more than one door," Anna said. "I took him through the side door and up the back stairway."

"The back stairway?" Harper narrowed her eyes. "We saw the footprint in the dust in the hallway. If Anna brought Eric in through another door and approached the ward from a different direction, who did that footprint belong to?"

"That's a very good question," Jared said. "We have a few other issues to discuss while we're pondering that." He strode to the door, looked both ways down the hallway before returning to the bed. "We have a new set of problems to deal with. The first is that now we know that backup isn't coming today."

"I'm sorry about that." Eric lowered his gaze. "We should've powered through."

"It wouldn't have helped anyone if you guys got lost," Jared argued. "You did what you thought was right and now isn't the time to second guess yourself for that. What's done is done."

"He's right," Zander said. "If you got turned around on the lake you could've ended up in Canada without realizing it. We would've been worse off for that. The boat isn't overly large either. It might've sunk on the open lake."

"Oh, well, that makes me feel much better," Eric said dryly.

Harper patted his arm reassuringly. "It's okay. We're just glad you're all right. When we found the boat empty we weren't sure what to think."

"And we still don't know what happened to John," Jared added. "I think we can all agree that someone human is doing the bulk of this. Eric didn't hit himself from behind. That means someone else did it.

"Now, John would be the obvious culprit because we know he was out there on the boat at one time," he continued. "I can't rule him out as an accomplice – it's entirely possible we're dealing with a team rather than one person – but I think someone in the group that remained behind has to be involved."

"Because of the way Molly disappeared?" Zander asked.

Jared didn't get a chance to answer, in fact he was mid-nod when Eric bolted to a sitting position and dug his fingers into Zander's forearm. "Lay down or you'll make yourself sick," Jared ordered.

Eric ignored him. "What do you mean? Molly disappeared? But ... how?"

Harper's heart pinched at the horrified look on Eric's face. "It happened while we were sleeping. She was in a sleeping bag next to Zander and Shawn when we fell asleep but ... she wasn't there when we woke up."

"That's how we found the boat in the first place," Jared said. "We were outside looking for her."

"You lost her?" Eric's voice took on a hard edge. "How could you do that?"

"It's not as if we did it on purpose," Zander protested. "She was there when we went to bed."

"And yet the four of you are perfectly fine," Eric snapped. "Let me guess, you guys were all wrapped up in each other and she was left alone. You guys slept wrapped around each other, didn't you? You couldn't be bothered to notice the poor girl who was left on her own."

Jared bit back an angry retort. "We did our best. We didn't know this would happen."

"Uh-huh." Eric wasn't convinced. "Let me ask you something, Jared, if I'd been left in charge and Harper went missing in the middle of the night, how would you feel right about now?"

"I would probably kill you," Jared replied calmly. "That doesn't change the fact that this is the last thing we wanted and we're doing our best to find Molly."

"Really? It looks to me as if you're all sitting around." Eric crossed his arms over his chest, his fury evident. "I shouldn't have left her. I should have taken her with me."

Zander narrowed his eyes, suspicious. "You know, now that we've found you, something was brought to our attention a few hours ago. We wanted to ignore it, pretend it wasn't true, but I'm starting to think those idiot camera operators had a point."

"I'm starting to think they did, too," Harper acknowledged, pinning an increasingly distraught Eric with a hard gaze. "Are you and Molly involved?"

"What? We're co-workers," Eric protested, averting his gaze.

"Are you co-workers who occasionally kiss?" Zander pressed.

It wasn't a funny situation, but Harper couldn't stop herself from cracking a smile when Eric's face flooded with color.

"You are." Harper couldn't decide if the news made her happy or sad. Molly had been after Eric for so long she lost count of the times she bought the girl ice cream to soothe her frazzled nerves when Eric refused to notice her. "When did this happen?"

"When you guys were caught up with your new boyfriends," Eric spat, shaking his head. "It was just one of those ... things. We went to a bar one night to complain about how you never remember to include us and one thing led to another."

"And then you had second thoughts because she's younger than you," Jared volunteered. "That's why you guys were sniping at one another. You pulled back and hurt her feelings."

Eric nodded, morose. "And then I left her and she ... ." He broke off on a strangled sob.

"We're going to find her," Jared said, leaning forward and resting his hand on Eric's shoulder. "We were actually up here looking for her when we found you. We'll get right back to it."

"We should probably take Eric downstairs so he can rest in the foyer," Zander said. "He's not strong enough to go with us."

"Screw that," Eric snapped. "I'm going with you. I have to ... I have to apologize. She has to know I didn't mean what I said."

Harper was curious to know what he said, but now wasn't the time to press him on it. "You can't come with us. You're sick and you'll probably have a bit of vertigo. You need to rest. However, I don't think taking him to the main floor is a good idea."

"Why not?" Zander asked.

"Because someone thinks that he's out of the picture," Jared answered. "They don't think that he's a concern. If that individual realizes that he's still alive, that he might be able to identify his assailant, then Eric might become a target a second time. We have to keep him buttoned up."

"No way," Eric argued. "I want to find Molly. I ... need ... to find her."

"We're going to find her and bring her to you," Jared said, his eyes serious as they locked with Eric's miserable orbs. "I swear to you that I won't let you down a second time."

"I think that means that Eric should stay here," Shawn said. "He was obviously safe here overnight. I think he'll be safe a bit longer, although he shouldn't stay alone."

"Definitely not," Jared agreed. "In fact ... Harper is going to stay with him."

Harper balked. "What? You just spent twenty minutes explaining how we were all going to stay together as a group. Now you want to separate?"

"Now I want you safe," Jared corrected. "I think you're safe here. Anna brought Eric here for a reason."

"No one ever comes in here," Anna supplied. "I don't know if it's because of the fact that it was the children's ward, but it's mostly empty. Only a few souls ever breach the walls."

"That doesn't change the fact that I can't stay here," Harper said, adopting a pragmatic approach. "Forget the fact that Jared swore up and down he wouldn't be separated from me – which I won't forget, mind you – but you can't find Molly without me."

"And why is that?" Jared asked, planting his hands on his hips. He was ready for a fight should it come to it. He truly believed Harper would be safe if she stayed with Eric. That was the most important thing to him.

"Because you need me to converse with ghosts in case they can help us," Harper fired back. "Unless you've suddenly become a conduit without me knowing, I have to be a part of your team."

Jared worked his jaw, Harper's smug expression setting his teeth on edge. He wanted to argue with her assessment, but she was right.

"Oh, she rendered him speechless," Zander said, grinning. "I wasn't sure that was even possible."

"I'm not fond of any of you right now," Jared gritted out. "I can't come up with one single thing to trump what she said, though."

Harper beamed as she patted his arm. She'd already won. They both knew it. "That means someone else is going to have to stay with Eric and you're going to have to listen to me crow about being right until the end of time."

Jared pursed his lips to keep from laughing. He didn't want to encourage her. "I'm willing to put up with that for the time being. We still don't know where to start looking for Molly, though, so I wouldn't get too smug."

"I know where to look for her," Anna offered. "In fact, I think I know exactly where she is."

And just like that, a new search was afoot.

## ❧ 18 ❧

## EIGHTEEN

U ltimately it was decided that Shawn would stay behind with Eric. The reasoning was vague – and Jared would've much preferred to leave Zander behind – but eventually he realized that separating Zander and Harper was a bad idea because it would leave both of them with degraded focus.

"Where are you taking us?" Harper asked, doing her best to ignore the way Jared and Zander crowded her as she followed Anna toward the end of the hallway. "Do you know where you're going?"

"I think she knows where she's going," Zander noted. "She's lived here for decades. I would trust her sense of direction over yours any day of the week."

"What is that supposed to mean?"

"You know what it means." Zander was unruffled. "I'm sure you remember the time you navigated us to that hunting shack in the middle of nowhere and we found that 'hunting' was really code for cross-dressing that one time."

Jared was interested despite himself. "You found cross-dressing hunters in Michigan? Do tell."

"It wasn't as bad as he makes it sound," Harper said, keeping Anna firmly in sight as she rolled her neck. "I accidentally transposed two of the address numbers and we ended up at the wrong cabin. The owner was very nice when we explained the error."

"He was also wearing a frilly apron and nothing else," Zander noted. "That includes underwear."

"It was a hot day," Harper argued. "He didn't have air conditioning and he wasn't keen to sweat in certain places if he didn't have to. I don't think he was a cross-dresser as much as a nudist."

"I see." Jared smirked. "You guys sound like you get very little work done when you're on a case."

"That's not true," Zander countered. "We get a lot of work done. It's just not always done in a linear fashion."

"Good to know." Jared's fingers itched to link with Harper's, but he fought the urge because he didn't want her to think he was overbearing. "Do we have any idea where we're going yet?"

"Anna apparently isn't feeling chatty," Harper replied. "We're just following her right now."

"So she could be leading us to a horrible death. That's what you're saying, right?"

Harper shrugged. "At least we'll be together."

Jared didn't miss the pointed statement. "I didn't want to leave you behind just to leave you behind. That's not why I suggested it."

"That's not how it felt," Harper sniffed.

"Stop being difficult, Harp," Zander chided. "He was trying to protect you. He shouldn't be shamed for it."

"Thank you, Zander." Jared was surprised and thankful for the backup. "I appreciate you taking my side on this."

"Oh, I'm not taking your side," Zander clarified. "I'm simply pointing out that I understand what you were trying to do. I don't think it was right."

Jared's smile slipped. "You make me tired."

"Right back at you." Zander winked, a gesture that caused Jared's jaw to tighten. "I admire the fact that you want to keep her safe, but we've been taking care of ourselves for a very long time. We don't need constant parental guidance."

"That's not what I was doing," Jared protested. "Wait ... is that how you see me? Am I the dad in all of this?"

"That's not how I see you," Harper replied. "Not only would that be gross and wrong, but I don't see you as a constant killjoy. That's Zander's thing."

"I don't know whether to thank you or stop listening to this conversation," Jared muttered.

"I would thank me," Harper said. "As for what happened upstairs, I understand why you did it, too. That doesn't mean I agree with it or appreciate the fact that you tried to cut me out of my own investigation, but I understand it."

"Maybe we should stop talking for five minutes or so," Jared suggested. "My head is starting to hurt."

"I think that's a fine idea," Zander said. "That will allow Harper and me a chance to talk about the big pink elephant in the room."

"You mean Eric and Molly?" Harper scratched her cheek as Anna led them to a rickety looking spiral staircase. "Yeah, I'm a little upset that we didn't notice either. Do you think that means we're self-involved?"

"Of course not. We have giving hearts."

"That doesn't mean we're not self-involved."

"True," Zander conceded. "If we admit to being self-involved, though, it's a label we'll never be able to shake. I prefer to think of us as distracted. It's not our fault that we found unique and intriguing mates at the same time."

"Just for the record, I'm not okay when you use the word 'mate' to refer to me," Jared interjected. "It makes me think of animals."

"If the paw print fits," Zander teased. "I thought you were going to be quiet for five minutes, by the way."

"I forgot. Continue."

"So, what were we talking about?" Zander turned an inquisitive look to Harper, but she was too busy glaring at the staircase. "Hmm. That doesn't exactly look safe."

"It's the only way to hit the far side of the institution," Anna supplied. "They designed it this way on purpose. You have to trust me."

Harper relayed the information and then moved to descend. Jared swiftly cut her off.

"I think we should go down one at a time so we don't tax that thing," Jared said. "Just to be on the safe side."

"Okay." Harper started to move again, but Jared shook his head.

"I will go first," Jared said. "You will go after me and Zander will bring up the rear."

"I don't like what that implies," Zander groused.

Jared ignored his tone. "If you want to go first, Zander, be my guest. Just remember we have no idea what – or who, for that matter – is down there."

Zander swallowed hard. "You go first. I like bringing up the rear."

Harper snickered as Jared gave her a hasty kiss.

"I'll be quick and call up as soon as it's okay for you to come down."

Harper nodded. "Okay." She watched as Jared descended, her heart rate picking up a notch, although she had no idea why. The staircase rattled as Jared progressed, and it took him almost a full minute to hit the floor beneath.

"It's okay, Heart," he called out. "It's rickety, but you'll be okay."

Harper spared a glance for Zander and forced a smile. "Don't take too long bringing up the rear."

Zander risked a glance over his shoulder, the lonely darkness causing him to shudder. "Don't worry about that."

Harper sucked in a breath and started down, increasing her pace when she imagined Zander sitting on the second floor alone. She'd barely hit the floor when she called up for Zander to follow and he almost ran down he was so worked up. He threw his arms around Harper's neck, catching Jared in the process, and heaved out a relieved sigh.

"We made it."

Jared shook his head as he placed his palm on the small of Harper's back. "We're a crack team of paranormal investigators, aren't we?"

Harper ignored the jibe and focused on Anna. "Where is this?"

"The back of the institution," Anna replied, resuming her trek. "We weren't allowed down here when we were alive. I didn't realize it existed until after I died."

"And what's down here?"

"Mostly office space."

Something occurred to Harper. "Dr. Bennett's office space?"

Anna nodded and pointed. "It's right over there."

Harper retrieved her flashlight from her pocket and switched it on, narrowing her eyes at the closed door. She didn't hesitate when she strode forward and tried the handle, looking to Jared for approval before pushing it open.

"It won't hurt to look," Jared said. "Let's see what's inside."

Zander was relieved when they pushed into the small room and found a window on the wall. He strode to it, yanking on the curtains as Shawn had upstairs. They ripped with little complaint. "Hmm. We're on the south side of the building. I can't see the boat or the dock."

"This wasn't on the plans, was it?" Jared searched his memory. "Did you see office space on the plans?"

"No." Harper moved to the filing cabinet behind the desk, sparing a moment to stare at the faded and disintegrating framed photograph on top of the rectangular piece of furniture. She recognized the man in it from her vision the previous day. John Jacob Bennett. "I'm starting to think quite a bit of this building wasn't on the plans. There has to be a reason for that."

"And what do you think the reason is?"

Harper shrugged as she thumbed through the faded files. The filing cabinet, metal like the one upstairs, had kept the files inside remarkably dry. "Here's your file, Anna."

Anna floated closer to Harper and watched as the blonde tilted her flashlight so she could read through the pages.

"Anything?" Jared asked after a few minutes.

"It's mostly the same thing as upstairs, although there is a notation in this one that seems to indicate that Anna's baby was handed off to his father," Harper replied. "It was a boy, eight pounds and seven ounces. He was healthy and the father paid a fee to the institution when he took custody."

"A fee?" Jared cocked an eyebrow. "What kind of fee?"

"Five hundred dollars."

"For?"

"It doesn't say, but I'm betting that Gerard Hicks wasn't the only one to give money to the institute to make a problem go away,"

Harper said, lifting her eyes as she sorted through the possibilities. "I mean ... think about it. Anna was supposed to be released to her parents' care once she gave birth. Instead she was forced to remain here.

"This file has little red notations every six months," she continued. "I've seen Zander make similar notations in our files."

"Let me see." Zander leaned over so he could get a closer look. "That seems to indicate that someone was paying money to the institute every six months and it was being credited to Anna's account. I can't really read the amounts, though, because they're smudged."

"Were your parents paying for you to be kept here, Anna?" Harper asked.

Anna shook her head. "They didn't have extra money. That's why they wanted me to get married. They thought I was a drain on their finances."

"But they agreed for you to be sent here," Harper pressed. "Someone had to pay to make that happen. I'm going to guess it was Hicks. He's the one who had the most to lose if people found out you gave birth to his son."

"Do you think he's the one who paid to keep her here?" Zander asked.

"It's the only thing that makes sense to me," Harper replied. "Bennett fled after the state came in and seized control of the institution. He had to know they would find some hinky stuff here."

"It sounds like he had enough money – between what he was getting here and what his parents had – to probably flee the country," Jared added. "This place might've been actually worse than we originally thought."

"I'm not sure how much worse it could get," Zander said.

"What if they were using it to launder money at the same time they were doing stuff to the patients?" Jared challenged. "I mean ... think about it. The Bennett family was rich and it sounds as if the son might've been a psychopath."

"It was the best of both worlds," Harper mused. "He could experiment – do whatever terrible things he wanted to do – and make money at the same time. Then, when he realized his playpen was about to get taken away from him, he took off to parts unknown. He probably set up shop under a different name or something."

"That makes sense to me," Jared said. "We can do some research when we get back to Whisper Cove, but I'm going to bet that those records are so far buried we'll never find them."

"What about my baby, though?" Anna asked. "Do you really think he survived?"

Harper knew what she was asking and took pity on her. "I wasn't certain when you first told me your story," she hedged. "I do think that the baby went to his father, though. You said that the father and his wife didn't have any children of their own. Maybe they couldn't. I'm going to wager they took the baby and raised it together."

"How would that work?" Zander asked. "Wouldn't the wife have been irritated to find out that her husband not only had a baby with someone else, but that she was supposed to take care of it?"

"Sure," Harper confirmed. "But what if he didn't tell her it was his baby? What if he just suddenly showed up with a baby one day and they happened to be lucky enough to adopt it? Bennett had everything he needed here to fake a birth certificate and name someone else as the mother."

"That's diabolical, but I can totally see it happening," Zander said. "Would he still be alive?"

Harper did the math in her head. "He would be seventy-seven. He could very well be alive."

"Seventy-seven?" Anna widened her eyes. "Are you sure?"

"Sadly, yes." Harper's smile was wan. "You've been imagining him as a baby all of this time, haven't you?"

"I don't spend a lot of time daydreaming, but he never advanced in age in my head," Anna said. "Then, after I died, I guess I never advanced in age either. That's kind of sad, isn't it?"

"It's unbelievably sad," Harper confirmed, shifting so she could rest a hip against the corner of the desk. "Your son, if he's still alive, could have children and grandchildren of his own, though. That's kind of exciting to think about, isn't it?"

Anna shrugged. "Grandchildren and great-grandchildren are something I never considered. I just always wanted him."

Harper's stomach twisted. "I'm sorry."

"Why? You didn't do anything." Anna turned to stare out the window. "You said you could help me move on. Is that true?"

"Yes."

"Do you think my son will be there?"

"I don't know," Harper replied, opting for honesty. "He could still be alive. If he is, though, you could be waiting for him over there and I'm sure he'll be happy to see you when it's your time. You don't have to stay here."

Jared could sense Harper's distress so he ran his hand over her shoulder in an effort to soothe her.

"I'll consider it." Anna's lips curved. "You probably want to find your friend now, right?"

"I do." Harper bobbed her head. "Do you know where she's at?"

"No, but I'm going to guess she's with the other woman who went missing in the basement."

Harper stilled. "Lucy?"

"What is she saying?" Jared asked.

Harper energetically waved her hand to silence him. "Did you see Lucy after she disappeared?"

"I did." Anna either didn't understand the shift in Harper's demeanor or didn't register it. "She was in the basement with a small ... I don't know what it was, square thing or something ... in her hand."

"She had a square thing in her hand?" Harper asked, furrowing her brow.

"It must have been a camera," Zander said. "She was probably going to film her own little side adventure, complete with you showing up to find her, Harp."

"Probably. What happened after that, Anna?"

"Someone found her."

"Who?"

"Someone bad." Anna's voice was barely a whisper. "She tried to hide, but it was too late."

Harper's stomach did an inelegant somersault. "Is she dead?"

"I don't know. I couldn't really see the man who came for her because I was distracted by ... something. She's in the dark place, though. I know that."

"Is that a technical term?"

"What did she say?" Jared asked, his impatience bubbling to the forefront.

"She said that Lucy is in the dark place," Harper replied. "She was in the basement and someone came down, although she doesn't know who. She doesn't know if Lucy is dead but assumes that Molly is with her."

"Then that's where we have to go," Jared said, getting to his feet. "Take us to the dark place, Anna."

"Of course." Anna drifted toward the door. "If your friend dies here, most likely she will come back and be like me. That's what happens to most of them."

"Most of who?"

"The ones who die here," Anna replied. "Even the newer ones. They all stay."

Something niggled at the back of Harper's brain. "Has someone died here recently?"

"Two someones," Anna answered. "Julie and Ashley. They're part of the group now."

"Julie?" Harper instinctively reached into Jared's pocket and tugged out the bracelet he shoved there after they discovered it on the beach. She held her flashlight so she could read the name on it a second time. "This Julie?"

"Yes," Anna said. "She was in the dark place, too. Now she's in a different dark place."

Harper briefly pressed her eyes shut. "I'm starting to think this dark place is right out of a nightmare."

"You're not far off."

## ❦ 19 ❧

# NINETEEN

H arper was quiet as Anna led them through the hallway, flashlights on. Everyone was quiet, in fact. It was almost as if they realized they were very close to the end and they didn't want to risk making a mistake that would turn the tide in favor of the wrong faction.

When they reached a second spiral staircase, Jared growled as he tilted his flashlight to search the floor beneath. "This leads to the basement." It wasn't really a question. "We already searched the basement."

"Not the part with the dark place," Anna murmured.

"I'm guessing that there's a section of the basement that's only accessible through these back staircases, too," Harper said. "We have to look, Jared."

"I know we do, Heart." Jared wasn't disputing that assumption. "I just don't like the idea of being separated, even if it's only for a minute."

"Let's just get it over with."

They went down in the same configuration. This time when Harper hit the basement floor Jared was waiting and grabbed her hand. Once Zander joined the crowd, he hooked his finger through one of Harper's belt loops and pressed his body close to hers.

"How close?" Zander asked, his voice breathy with excitement and fear.

"Very close," Anna replied. "In fact, it's right over there."

Harper mimicked the way Anna pointed so Jared and Zander would know where they were headed. They took one step together in tandem before the sound of a slamming door caused them to jolt in unison.

Jared's eyes widened and he immediately flicked off his flashlight. Harper and Zander followed suit, more out of instinct than anything else, and for a long beat all they heard was a trio of raspy breaths as they waited for something to happen. The silence stretched into what felt like eternity and Jared was just about ready to turn on his flashlight when the unmistakable sound of echoing footsteps assailed his ears.

He reacted quickly, grabbing Harper around the waist and dragging her to the wall so they could crouch down behind an abandoned metal rack. Zander wisely stayed on the other side of the hallway so he could hunker behind an old linen cart, although he wasn't happy about being separated from his best friend.

Jared positioned Harper so she was on her knees, his chest to her back, and calmly stroked her hair to calm her. He stared down the hallway — which thankfully wasn't very long — and narrowed his eyes when a flashlight beam danced along the tiled floor at the intersection where the two hallways met. He lifted a finger to his lips to warn Zander to be quiet, earning an "I'm not stupid" look for his efforts, and then returned to waiting for their mystery guest to show himself.

The flashlight beam got bigger, the footsteps louder, and finally a dark figure appeared in the spot where the two hallways met. Jared's breathing was even as he debated what would happen next. If the shadow moved down their hallway he would have no choice but to attack. The figure would probably make it to them without realizing they were there, but once they were even it would be over. Once Jared launched himself at their foe, though, that would give Zander and Harper a chance to escape ... maybe even get into this dark place and find Molly and Lucy.

Of course, that meant Harper and Zander would have to leave him behind. The odds of Harper doing something rational like leaving him to fight his own battle seemed slim given the circumstances.

"If he comes down here, I'm going to distract him. That means you have to run with Zander." Jared's words were barely a whisper against Harper's ear.

She shook her head, keeping her eyes focused forward.

"You have to," Jared pressed.

"I won't."

Harper's voice was a bit louder than Jared's and he jerked his chin up to see if the man – and it was clearly a man given the broad shoulders and triangle-shaped torso – heard. The shadow didn't so much as glance in their direction.

"You'll have to," Jared said. "I'll be okay, but I need to know you're safe."

"No."

"Dammit, Heart." This time it was Jared who spoke a little too loudly. Thankfully for him the shadow opted to continue walking down the other hallway, leaving them to their hiding places.

Jared opened his mouth to chastise Harper further but stopped when he heard their mystery guest fumbling with a door. He arched an eyebrow and held up a finger, indicating Harper should wait where she was. He gave Zander the same silent order and then planted his hands and knees on the grimy tile so he could crawl forward and see better.

Jared didn't consider himself squeamish by nature, but he had a feeling the floor was not only dirty but littered with the carcasses of insects he'd rather never touch. He did his best to push the idea out of his mind as he approached the end of the hallway, ducking behind a misshapen lump that he assumed was once a fabric chair of some sort. Water and decay had turned it into something else. Sadly, he had a feeling that something else was home to creepy-crawly things, but he ignored the urge to run away screaming.

It was hard to see down the second hallway. The basement offered no ambient light, the emergency lights on the walls long since dead. The only illumination came from the flashlight the man carried, and even though he was much closer now Jared had trouble making out the individual's features. All he could say with any degree of certainty was that it wasn't Steve. Steve was much taller and broader. It could be anyone else in their group, though.

Jared maintained an easy breathing rhythm as the man opened the door across the way and stepped inside. Jared took advantage of the situation to crawl forward, look both ways down the hallway, and then return to his hiding spot before the man hit the hallway again. The dark figure made no noise other than the normal sounds of oxygen intake and feet shuffling against the floor.

Jared held in a long breath when the shadow moved past the spot where he hid, but there was no hesitation or long probing gazes to indicate that the figure suspected he was being watched. Jared remained exactly where he was for a long time, listening to the echo of footsteps until they were nothing but a memory.

When he turned to return to Harper, he found her crouched on the floor behind him, flashlight switched on and pointed toward her pretty face, so close they almost bumped chins when he put his head down.

"Do you ever listen to what I tell you to do?" Jared hissed, forcing himself to remain calm despite the way his heart skipped a beat. "You scared the crap out of me."

Harper merely tilted her head to the side. "Do you want me to hold your hand so you feel better?"

Jared scowled. "You and I are going to have a long talk about what happens when we're in a dangerous situation when we get back to Whisper Cove." Jared kept his voice low even though he was fairly sure the dark figure was gone. "You seem to forget that I'm the boss in situations like this."

Harper didn't bother to hide her eye roll. "When have we ever been in a situation like this?"

Zander, who came out of his hiding spot and joined the couple because he was sick of being alone, raised his hand. "We're in situations like this all of the time. Just a few weeks ago, for example, we hid under a table in a dentist's office while he was trying to kill us."

Jared scowled. "I remember. I wanted to kill you both that day, too."

"And yet we're still alive." Harper patted Jared's forearm. "There's something in that room. We need to see what it is. That's the place Anna called the dark room before she disappeared."

"She disappeared?" Jared wasn't happy with the news. "Where did she go?"

Harper held her hands palms up and shrugged. "I don't know. I couldn't very well ask her. Did you see who that was?"

Jared shook his head. "It's not Steve. I'm sure of that."

"So you ruled out one guy?" Zander wasn't impressed. "That's not very good police work."

"Remind me to never work with you guys again," Jared muttered, turning his attention back toward the room. "We need to get in there."

"That's the plan," Harper agreed, giving him a small shove. "Get to it."

"Don't get bossy." Jared wagged a finger, surprising Harper with a quick kiss before turning to the room. He got to his feet, casting a long and weighted look down the hallway in the direction the figure disappeared, and then moved to the door. Zander and Harper weren't far behind – refusing to be cut out of a potential rescue (or trouble, should Jared find something truly terrible behind the door) – and everyone sucked in breaths of anticipation as Jared twisted the handle.

Nothing happened.

Jared tried it again, but the handle wouldn't budge.

"Oh, man, that was anticlimactic," Zander complained, rolling his neck until it cracked. "I thought we would open the door, gasp at the same time, and then save the day. This totally bites."

Harper arched an eyebrow, his commentary serving as a way to lighten the heavy mood. "Maybe next time."

"A guy can hope."

"You guys are just messing with me now," Jared muttered, tugging at the handle. "It's locked."

"You're certainly a master of the obvious," Zander quipped, digging in his pocket and returning with the lock-picking set Harper used the day before. "Show him how it's done, Harp."

Jared was dumbfounded. "Why did you bring that?"

"Because a Boy Scout is always prepared."

Harper took the set and grabbed the tools she needed. "You were never a Boy Scout. You hated the polyester."

"I was a Boy Scout at heart if not in practice," Zander countered. "The polyester really was a deal breaker, though."

"So was the camping because you hate bugs." Harper knelt and gestured with her hand so Jared knew where to hold the flashlight beam. "I'm surprised you agreed to do this since it involved camping."

"I did this for you." Zander said the words quickly, realizing too late that he should have kept them to himself. When he risked a glance at Harper he found her staring at him, mouth gaping. "What?"

"You didn't do this for me," Harper argued. "You did this for you."

"Keep opening that lock while you're arguing," Jared ordered, prodding Harper to return to her task. "We're going to talk about how you carry a lock-picking kit around with you while on a job, by the way. That's going on the list of serious discussions we're going to have when we get back to Whisper Cove."

"*If* we get back to Whisper Cove," Harper muttered, her eyes flashing dark.

"We're getting back," Jared said, his expression earnest. "In fact, hopefully we're going back in the next hour. If Molly and Lucy are on the other side of this door, there's absolutely nothing stopping us from rescuing them, grabbing Eric and Shawn from the second floor, and going for help."

Harper stared at him for a long beat, her fingers unmoving. "What about John?"

"We'll get help," Jared replied. "If Molly is in here, we're going. We'll come back with help — heck, I'll come back with the Coast Guard if I have to — but we're leaving if we find Molly."

Harper swallowed hard and nodded before turning back to her task. "I miss sleeping in a bed."

"I miss waking up with you in a bed," Jared groused. "Heck, I miss waking up with both of you."

Harper smirked at the admission as Zander puffed out his chest. It took her a moment to remember what they were talking about before Jared distracted her, though, and when she turned the conversation back to Zander's announcement, her tone was accusatory. "You did not do this for me, by the way. I did it for you because you wanted to be on television."

Zander balked. "That is not true."

"It's totally true."

"It is not!"

"It is and there's no reason to argue about it," Jared interjected. "You wanted to be on television. I could've convinced Harper to let me take her to this island if it wasn't for you and that stupid television show."

"And why would you want to do that?" Zander asked.

"Because I didn't like the idea from the beginning, but I wanted to be supportive," Jared replied, not missing a beat. "I love Harper. I want her to have everything she wants. She didn't want to be on television, but she did want to see this asylum – even though she feared it – and she did want to make you happy. So that's what we did."

Zander's face was stark white in the limited light. "But ... I thought you wanted to do this, Harp. I thought it was something fun we could do together."

"I wanted to see the asylum," Harper admitted, gritting her teeth as she fiddled with the lock. "I don't care about television, though. You wanted it so I wanted it for you."

"We all want the best for each other," Jared said, grinning. "We're good and loving people."

"Shut up." Zander flicked Jared's ear. "You should have told me she didn't want to be here."

"I thought you knew," Jared said, ruefully rubbing his ear. "You read her better than most people – better than me at times – and it was obvious when I looked at her. She was curious and miserable at the same time. It was written all over her face."

"But ... ." Zander broke off, searching his memory. "Oh, well, this bites. I kind of wanted to be on television, but I would've totally abandoned the idea if I knew it made you unhappy. I love you more than the idea of being famous, Harp."

"I know that." Harper offered up a fleeting smile. "It's okay. I'm not sorry we came."

"Really?" Jared cocked a dubious eyebrow. "After all of this, you're not sorry?"

"I'm not happy, but if we can help Anna and a few of the others, I won't be sorry. I ... got it!" The sound of the lock snicking into place caused Harper to hop to her feet. She pocketed the lock pick tools and watched as Jared twisted the door handle.

The door popped open with only a loud squeak of protest. Jared was back to being serious so he lifted a finger to still Harper and Zander and stepped into the room. He was slow and methodical as he bounced his flashlight around the dank space, stopping when he caught a hint of movement in the far corner.

Harper followed his gaze, crying out and bolting forward when she recognized Molly's green head. "Molly!"

"Harper?"

Molly was so relieved when she saw her boss that she burst into tears, struggling to get to her feet as Harper approached. Harper threw her arms around Molly's neck, ignoring the way the girl fought to stand.

"We've been so worried," Harper said, fighting off her own set of tears. "We thought ... I don't know what we thought, but it wasn't good. How did you end up here?"

"I went to the bathroom after everyone was asleep last night," Molly replied. "Someone came up behind me and ... well, it was over pretty quickly. When I woke up I was in here."

"Are you alone?" Jared asked, furrowing his brow as he tried to search the room. "Is Lucy with you?"

"She was," Molly said, her voice wavering. "She passed out about two hours ago. I ... she hasn't woken up again."

"Where?"

"Here." Molly lifted the nearby blanket, revealing the prone form of Lucy. The woman was unnaturally pale, her breath coming in shallow gasps. She didn't look well. "I think she's dying."

"What happened to her?" Jared asked, pressing his hand to Lucy's neck to check for a pulse as he knelt. "Was she hit over the head ... or did something else happen?"

"She was drugged with whatever stuff I was – I think it was chloroform – but she was stronger when I got here," Molly replied. "She went downhill fast."

"What does that mean?" Terror clawed through Harper's chest. "What's wrong with her?"

"I'm not sure," Jared muttered, slipping an arm under Lucy in an effort to lift her. "We need to get her out of here. I can carry her out, but that means you're going to have to help Molly, Zander."

Zander bobbed his head. "No problem." He leaned down to hook his hands under Molly's armpits but drew back when the younger woman's body went rigid. "What's wrong?"

Molly's eyes were fixed on the door, her lip quivering, causing Harper and Zander to expectantly snap their heads in that direction.

"He's back," Molly whispered. "He's back and ... he's not happy."

## 20

# TWENTY

H arper clutched her flashlight to her chest, fear gripping her belly. Zander let loose with a low whimper as he tugged Molly protectively to his side. Jared was the exact opposite, quickly standing and fixing his flashlight beam on the figure in the open doorway.

"Finn." Harper exhaled heavily, her mind working overtime as she tried to put the pieces of the puzzle together. She wasn't sure who she suspected – it easily could've been any of the men, after all – but Finn wasn't on the top of her list. "Why?"

Finn didn't appear surprised to find his prison infiltrated by inter-lopers. His face was impassive, although a glint of mayhem flitted through his eyes. "Why what? I was just passing by and heard voices. I'm here to help." His tone was flat, unconvincing. "Do you need help? I can carry Lucy."

"I don't think that's a good idea," Jared countered, moving a bit so he stood in front of Lucy should Finn rush in that direction. Harper stood between Zander and Jared – and Jared would've preferred her location to be closer to his – but he didn't make a move in that direc-tion. "What are you doing down here, Finn?"

"We decided to break up and search the grounds," Finn replied. "I happened on this place and heard your voices. We should get these women out of here."

He sounded so calm, almost rational, that for a split-second Harper considered believing him. Then her pragmatic side took over.

"You happened upon this place?" she challenged. "How? It's only accessible through the stairwells on the far side of the building. You can't hit it from the main foyer without doing some hard searching ... and without the plans or a guide, it seems virtually impossible to me."

"Huh. I just walked through a door."

"What door?"

"It's down that way." Finn vaguely waved in the direction he disappeared to before they entered the room. "It wasn't hard at all."

Harper didn't believe him for a second. "Then how come you came to this room, unlocked it, looked inside, and then left again?"

"Excuse me?" For the first time since entering, Finn expressed actual surprise. "What do you mean?"

"We saw you," Jared supplied. "We were hiding in the other hallway. We saw you come in here."

"I see." Finn licked his lips. "I guess I can't really explain that, can I?" He sounded more amused than fearful. "I have to admit, I didn't expect to find you down here. I didn't have time to come up with an appropriate story. I'll do better next time."

"Next time?" Jared adjusted his grip on the flashlight, never moving the beam from Finn's lanky frame. "There's not going to be a next time."

"You think that, don't you?" Finn was back to being amused. "All I have to do is shut this door, lock you in, and leave you here. You'll die and I can pick another room for the second group. It's really not that difficult."

Harper didn't like Finn's matter-of-fact tone so she decided to direct his attention to her in case Jared tried to push things to a place that would hurt all of them. "Why, Finn? Why did you do this?"

"I'm not sure you're asking the right question." Finn drifted to his right, walking in front of an aged countertop. "It's not *why* did I do this. It's *why* didn't I do this sooner? It's been a very ... freeing ... experience."

Harper wasn't sure what to make of his answer. "Do you have a tie to this place? You said you used to live locally. You mentioned it to Zander. Are you a Bennett or something?"

"Not a Bennett, no." Finn smirked. "Never a Bennett."

Harper flicked her eyes to Anna when the ghost appeared in the doorway. She expected the woman to address her, but Anna's eyes were fixed on Finn. There was a sadness in their depths that Harper didn't have an easy time identifying.

"John Jacob Bennett moved to Malta after he fled Michigan, in case you're wondering," Finn offered. "I did quite a bit of research on this place when I found out we would be visiting. Actually, I did the research years before. I'm the one who tried to direct Michael here in the first place. It took a lot longer than I anticipated."

"He moved to Malta? That's a fine bit of investigative work." Harper hoped to appeal to Finn's ego as a distraction so Jared would have enough time to come up with a solid plan. "How did you find that out?"

"It wasn't difficult," Finn replied. "I had an interest in this place because my father told me about it before he died. He said some very bad things happened here. I grew up in the area – Dearborn, in fact – and I knew the legends. I started digging when I was still a teenager. I guess we have that in common, huh, Harper?"

Harper nodded without hesitation. "I guess we do. That still doesn't explain how you found out the information."

"My mother worked as a caterer for years before retiring," Finn answered, skimming his fingers over the counter as he paced back and forth. He was antsy but made no move to go after Jared, who was seemingly the biggest threat to whatever it was Finn had planned. "She knew the Bennett family. I worked for her part-time and on weekends while I was in high school and college, so when she hosted a party for the Bennetts I couldn't stop myself from asking questions."

"And they just told you?"

"No, that took a bit of liquor and some properly placed questions, but eventually I realized that they had several pieces of one-of-a-kind art. It all originated from Malta. Since every Bennett but one was accounted for, I asked the obvious question. CeeCee Bennett was drunk enough when I asked that she told me everything.

"John Jacob Bennett fled to Malta right after he left this place," he continued. "CeeCee, who would've been his niece, said that he wasn't to blame for anything that happened out here but knew he would get locked up. He claimed someone was framing him.

"I'm not sure she believed it, but she spouted the nonsense all the same," he said. "He lived out his days in Malta, never marrying. Whether or not he found trouble again, I don't know. I didn't care about him enough to dig that far."

"Why did you dig at all?" Harper asked, genuinely curious. "I know why I was interested. I wanted to know about the ghosts and I was certain there were a lot of them out here. Why were you so intrigued by this place?"

"Because it's where I started."

Harper stilled. "No. This place closed before you were even born. What are you ... thirty years old? Even if you're a young-looking forty-year-old, you still never spent time in this place while it was in operation."

"I'm thirty-two," Finn supplied. "And, no, I never spent time here back then. That's not what I said, though. I said this was where I started."

"I don't understand." Jared drew Finn's attention to him. "How could you have started here?"

Harper rolled her neck as Anna made an odd gesture. It was directed toward Finn, who couldn't see her, but Harper thought she might've understood it. "You're Anna Pritchard's grandson, aren't you?"

Jared shot Harper an odd look, although it was brief. "How can you possibly know that?"

"She can't," Finn answered. "She's just guessing."

"Maybe," Harper conceded. "I think Anna recognizes you, though. She seems to, at least."

Finn jerked his head to the side, as if searching for Anna's spirit. "She's here?"

"She is."

Finn's face split with an eerie grin. "I didn't know if the stories were true about you being able to see and talk to ghosts, but once you knew about Anna – once you found her records in the office – I knew you were the real deal.

"My mother sent me stories about you over the past few years," he continued. "You've earned something of a cult following in certain circles. I knew when I finally convinced Michael to visit the Ludington Asylum that you needed to be a part of our team."

"And why is that?"

"Because you're not a fake," Finn replied. "Most of the people we deal with are frauds and attention seekers. Not you, though. You only agreed to do it because you wanted to see the asylum. You were interested in the science of it all."

"That's not exactly true," Harper hedged. "I'm interested in helping the spirits move on. I guess that's mildly scientific, but it's more a matter of faith than anything else."

"I don't believe that, but it's hardly important." Finn stared at the spot where Anna's ghost watched him. Harper could almost imagine that he really saw her, but she knew he didn't. He might try to will himself to do it, but he wouldn't be successful. He didn't have "the gift."

"Go back to Anna," Jared ordered, his mind busy. "Are you saying you're her grandson?"

"I am." Finn beamed. "My father was her son. He told me when he got sick with cancer that he wasn't really a Hicks. I mean ... he was. I know that now. He always thought that Anna Pritchard gave birth to him and Gerard and Wendy Hicks adopted him out of the kindness of their hearts. He died not realizing that Hicks was his real father. I want to thank you for digging out that tidbit."

"What did his birth certificate say?" Harper asked.

"It listed Anna Pritchard as his birth mother and said she died in childbirth at this place," Finn replied. "I guess she lived a bit longer than that, although not much in the grand scheme of things."

"No, not much," Harper murmured. "I wonder if Bennett killed Anna Pritchard because of that. Maybe Anna's parents – her mother especially – decided to reclaim her at some point. If that happened,

Anna might recognize her own child with the Hicks. Bennett wouldn't risk that."

"That story makes as much sense as anything else," Finn acknowledged. "I tried to track down the Pritchards after I found out the truth. Anna's parents were long gone, of course, but Anna's cousin procreated and I managed to track down one of her children. Ned. He was a nice guy and he said that what happened with Anna was a tragedy. The family's official line was that Anna died in a car accident while taking care of a sick aunt in Iowa."

"Did he know the truth?"

"He did, but only because it was whispered about when he was a child," Finn answered. "He's dead now, too. He died about three years ago. I visited him on his deathbed – mostly because I was hoping he would be eager to unburden his soul – and he told me that Anna was pregnant and supposed to be at the asylum for six months at the most.

"When she didn't immediately return home, her parents made up a story about her settling out there, but Anna's mother was never happy with the turn of events," he continued. "When Anna's father died of a heart attack at an early age, her mother immediately started paperwork to get Anna out of this place. It obviously never happened."

"Because Bennett killed her." Harper stared at Anna. "You remember how it happened, don't you?"

"I just went to sleep," Anna replied, her voice weak. "I went into a room, he told me he had a new treatment plan, and I went to sleep."

Harper had a hard time believing a sadist like John Jacob Bennett would make it as easy as that, but she didn't put up a fight. If Anna didn't want to talk about her death, remember it even, she had no intention of pushing her.

"So you found out that you had a colorful past," Harper said, tipping her head so she could watch Finn resume his pacing. "Did you come out here when you were a kid?"

"I did." Finn smiled. "My friend Rod had a boat and we came out here. He was afraid, whiny, but I felt as if I was coming home."

"I'm guessing that's because he's off his rocker," Zander muttered. He'd remained largely silent for the bulk of the conversation, Molly tucked in quietly at his side as he calmed her, but his patience was clearly wearing thin.

Harper ignored his statement. "Did you visit more than once?"

"As often as I could manage, although Rod wasn't always keen because he said it was depressing," Finn replied. "Then I went to film school in California, changed my name because I never felt like a Hicks, and my life was different for a bit. I worked my way onto *Phantoms* at a certain point, though, and I knew that the show was the thing that would ultimately get me back here."

Jared let Harper ask the questions for a long stretch because Finn seemed to enjoy engaging with her. Now it was his turn to ask the hard questions. "Since you work for the production company, I'm going to guess that they sent people out here to scout the location before we landed. Michael did a good job of pretending this was the first time he'd seen the island in person, but that wasn't true, was it?"

"Actually it was," Finn countered, his eyes darkening as he pinned Jared with a taunting look. "Michael isn't one for manual labor. He goes to the locations, but only because he has to. I volunteered to scout this island myself."

"And it wasn't empty when you got here, was it?" Jared was putting things together at a fantastic rate. "There were kids partying out here when you arrived and it irritated you."

"I was already out here when the partiers arrived. I stayed inside, willing them to go away, but one of the girls was braver than the rest. She decided to see if she could look around."

"Julie," Jared muttered, shaking his head. "Where is she?"

"She wanted to know the truth of the building, so I showed it to her." Finn's crazy smile was back. "I don't think she got the truth of this place until the end. It was glorious when she realized it, though."

"The truth of this place?"

Finn smiled at Harper. "You understand, don't you? This place is immortal. Those who die within its walls come back. They're immortal. I'm giving people the gift of immortality when I take them here."

"That's not true," Harper countered, not caring in the least that she risked agitating Finn. She was almost to the point where she wanted to deafen herself with Q-tips just so she wouldn't have to listen to him talk for one second longer. "A place doesn't have power. It's the souls living inside — their strengths, their foibles, their weaknesses — that determine what happens in a place. The place itself is not powerful."

"You're wrong." Finn's voice went cold. "You're not looking at the situation correctly."

"Oh, I'm looking at it correctly and I'm pretty sure I have it all figured out," Harper said. "You're crazy. There's no getting around it. You're completely and totally mental and someone needs to lock you up and force feed you some meds."

"You take that back!"

Harper refused to shrink back despite the shift in Finn's tone. "You liked researching your genealogy — which isn't a bad thing — but it sparked something in your mind. You were never a normal kid and what you found out only made you worse."

"I am not crazy!" Finn was beside himself.

"You're worse than crazy," Harper argued. "You've convinced yourself that you're on a mission, that you're somehow doing good. You want to kill people here so they'll come back as ghosts — ghosts you can't even see, by the way, but maybe you have a touch of the gift and can feel them.

"You think this gives you power, but it really makes you a scared little boy," she continued. "You don't really care about creating spirits that live forever. You get off on the pain and suffering of your victims. You're nothing more than a garden-variety sociopath."

"I am not crazy!" Finn bellowed the words, clutching his hands at his sides as he took a step forward.

That was enough for Jared. He'd come to the same conclusion as Harper and he wasn't about to risk one more person falling to Finn's twisted wrath. "Don't you even think about touching her," Jared warned, cutting the distance between them. "I won't allow it."

"You don't have the power here," Finn scoffed. "I have the power. Me. This is my realm. This is my dark place. This is my ... destiny."

"Oh, shut up." Jared didn't bother ordering Finn to surrender, or try to talk him down. Instead he smashed his fist into the man's face, taking a bit of pleasure in watching Finn's head snap back as his eyes rolled to the back of his head. He went down hard, his body echoing against the tile as he flopped to a standstill.

Jared watched him for a long beat to see if he would move. When he didn't, he bent over and searched Finn's pockets until he came up with a key. He handed the key to a wide-eyed Harper before bending over to pick up Lucy.

"Is he dead?" Molly asked, her voice trembling.

"No," Jared replied. "He's just knocked out. "We're going to lock him in down here and take you guys upstairs. Then we're taking the boat to Whisper Cove and getting help. He'll be fine down here for a few hours. It's safer for us to know where he's at."

Molly blindly nodded. "Okay, but ... how are we going to get back to Whisper Cove without a boat? Eric and John left yesterday with the boat."

"They're back," Harper explained. "Well, at least Eric is. We're not sure what happened to John."

"Once I have backup, Finn is going to tell us what he did with John," Jared said darkly, cradling Lucy's limp form against his chest. "We're going to find him. I promise you that."

"Okay." Molly let Zander guide her toward the door. "Is Eric okay?"

"He has a concussion," Harper volunteered. "He's on the second floor with Shawn. He's angry ... and worried about you."

"Me?" Molly's eyes went wide. "Did he say he was worried about me?"

"He certainly did," Harper confirmed. "He also told us you two have become something of an item."

"And you're in big trouble for holding out on the gossip, missy," Zander barked with mock severity. "You know I don't like being the last one to hear about the gossip."

"I just want to see him," Molly admitted. "I'm not sure what there is to gossip about. He decided he didn't want to be with me after all."

"No, he didn't," Jared argued. "He got scared and said something stupid. Heck, knowing Eric, he probably said several stupid things. He regrets them now. Trust me."

"Did he say that?"

"Pretty much." Harper beamed. "I think you might get what you want after all."

"That's good." Molly managed a smile. "After today, I could use a few days of getting what I want."

"I think we all could," Jared said. "Come on, people. Let's get out of this place."

No one had to say it, but they all heartily agreed. The Ludington Asylum belonged in the past. Their futures were pointed in an entirely different direction.

# ❦ 21 ❦

## TWENTY-ONE

T en days later, they returned to the island.
Harper, Jared, Zander, and Shawn were the only ones present for the return voyage. Mel loaned them his boat – threatening Zander with deadly force should something happen to it – but he almost seemed glad to see them off.

This last bit of business weighed heavily on Harper and she wanted it done. When it was, she hoped to never again return to the Ludington Asylum. She knew that she would think about it, of course, even dream about it, but as for seeing it, this would be the last time.

"So what's going to happen to Finn?" Shawn asked, keeping close to Zander as they picked their way to the front door of the facility. The state police and Coast Guard banned travel to the island for more than a week as they collected evidence and discovered two bodies. One, Julie Newhart, had been missing from Canada for two weeks. That's why Michigan authorities hadn't heard about her disappearance. The other body remained unidentified, although Anna mentioned the name "Ashley" at one point, and Harper hoped she could get a last name to go with the first before leaving.

"He'll be charged with murder, kidnapping, assault, and whatever else they can pin on him," Jared replied. "I'll have to testify – you guys probably will, too – but the St. Clair County Sheriff's Department is taking over the bulk of the investigation."

"And what about Lucy?" Zander asked. "Have you heard how she's doing?"

"She was diabetic – something she apparently didn't want people to know because it affected her company insurance policy – and she was in desperate need of insulin by the time the paramedics arrived," Jared replied. "She was in a coma for a few days, but she's expected to make a full recovery."

"That's good." Zander didn't like the woman but that was hardly reason to wish ill will on her. "Did she say how Finn got her?"

"She took off on her own like we thought, but it was because she needed to inject herself with insulin and didn't want anyone to see," Jared explained. "When she was finished, she had a bit of juice but got turned around when she tried to come back. She swears up and down she wasn't trying to entice Harper into the basement."

"Do you believe her?"

"I don't know that it matters now, but I don't believe her," Jared said. "I think she did need her insulin, but I also think that she and Michael had a plan to draw Harper to the basement. Anna pretty much said as much to Harper, and she had no reason to lie. Finn probably stumbled across her when she was hiding and he put her in that room for safekeeping – I think he had plans to deal with her later – so Michael was legitimately confused when Lucy didn't pop back up."

"Well, Michael has his own set of problems," Harper said. "We withdrew consent for any of that footage to be aired and returned the money. If he tries to show it he's going to be sorry."

"Do you think he will?" Shawn asked.

"I think that he's worried about opening himself up to lawsuits more than anything, but I guess we'll have to wait and see." Harper shifted the bag she carried to her other arm so she could link her fingers with Jared's. "He has his hands full with the Finn situation because Julie Newhart's parents are making noise about suing. I don't think he'll be focusing on the footage any time soon."

"It won't bring back their daughter, but I hope they do sue," Jared said. "It might teach Michael a lesson."

"And John?" Shawn asked. "What about him?"

"He's still in the hospital," Jared replied. "He took a bad blow to the head on the beach and then got a bad bout of hypothermia. He says he recognized Finn on the beach that night – he came back like Eric suspected to talk to everyone – but Finn was behind him as they headed for the asylum and hit him with something. He's honestly lucky to be alive."

"The police found him in a small room down the same hallway where Finn was keeping Lucy and Molly," Harper added. "He was unconscious when they arrived but woke the next day and started talking."

"What about Trey?" Shawn asked. "Did he know what Finn was doing?"

"He claims he didn't and I have to believe him," Jared replied. "He's a complete and total jerk, but I don't think he was privy to the story. If he was, he would've used it to his advantage. The fact that he didn't tells me that he was in the dark."

"Just not the dark place," Harper murmured, gripping Jared's hand tighter.

Jared slid her a sidelong look. "How is Molly? I haven't seen her around the office the few times I've stopped in over the last week."

"We gave her some time off," Zander supplied. "She deserved it and ... well ... Eric is playing nursemaid."

The corners of Jared's mouth tipped up. "I see. Are they officially a couple?"

"They're not using those words, but when I stopped by with some gossip magazines and ice cream the other day, I caught them cuddling on the front porch," Harper said. "I think they're well on their way to being a couple. Eric might fight it a bit longer, but I don't think he'll have much luck."

"And Molly?"

"She's still traumatized. Eric says she's been having nightmares."

"Which means he's been spending the night," Zander pointed out. "Once they're both back at work full time, you'd better believe I'm going to get to the bottom of this story. I want to know exactly how it happened."

"I would expect nothing less." Jared slowed his pace when they reached the front door, giving Harper a searching look as she grabbed the strap of her bag. "Are you sure you want to do this?"

"There are a lot of spirits inside this place that want – no, need – to be set free," Harper replied. "We brought as many dreamcatchers as we could make in one week. I'm going to do what I promised to do."

"You could just help Anna and call it a day," he pointed out.

"I want to do more than that."

Jared understood. He knew she would say that. He gently tucked a strand of her blonde hair behind her ear. "We should get to it, right? We'll probably be here for the entire afternoon as it is."

"I brought lunch," Zander volunteered. "Chicken salad sandwiches, fresh fruit, and chocolate cake."

Harper brightened considerably. "How did you know I would want chocolate cake?"

"I've met you."

"Good point." Harper mustered a smile as she studied the building. It was small but genuine. "This is the best part of our job."

"Then I'm happy to see you in action," Jared said. "We need to go over the rules before we go inside, though."

Harper rolled her eyes. "I know. I'm not allowed to go anywhere alone because I'm a female and I need to be protected."

Jared shook his head. "No, you're not allowed to go anywhere alone because I'm scared of ghosts and need you to protect me."

Despite herself, Harper giggled. "That was a really good response."

"I meant it."

"That's almost better than chocolate cake."

"Don't ever hate on the cake," Zander warned. "Now, come on. We have souls to save and cake to eat."

"And then we'll say goodbye to this place," Harper said. "I'm not sorry I came – I'm really not – but I'll be happy to leave."

"I think it's safe to say that goes for all of us, Heart."

The four friends walked into the building together, hope fueling them instead of fear this time. It wasn't work that would make them famous, but it was definitely work that would leave them fulfilled.

For all of them, that was more than enough.

Made in the USA
Lexington, KY
20 June 2017